First published in Germany as *Gespensterpark. Die Geheimtür zur Geisterwelt*
and as *Gespensterpark. Der geheime Rat der Zwölf* by Verlag Friedrich Oetinger GmbH,
Hamburg 2002. Original text copyright © 2002 by Verlag Friedrich Oetinger GmbH.
English translation copyright © 2004 by Verlag Friedrich Oetinger GmbH.
Revised English translation copyright © 2007 by North-South Books Inc., New York.

First published in the United States, Great Britain, Canada, Australia, and New Zealand
in 2007 by North-South Books Inc., an imprint of NordSüd Verlag AG, Zürich,
Switzerland. Distributed in the United States by North-South Books Inc., New York.

Library of Congress Cataloging-in-Publication Data is available.
A CIP catalogue record for this book is available from The British Library.

ISBN-13: 978-0-7358-2099-9 / ISBN-10: 0-7358-2099-6 (trade edition)
10 9 8 7 6 5 4 3 2 1

Printed in Germany


Published in cooperation with Verlag Friedrich Oetinger GmbH, Hamburg, Germany.
German ISBN 978-3-86684-003-4

# Ghost Park

## Book I The Vanishing Gate
## Book II The Imposter

By Marliese Arold
Illustrated by Barbara Scholz
Translated by Alexis L. Spry

NORTHSOUTH
BOOKS
New York / London

# Contents

Book I

# The Vanishing Gate

# The Mysterious Advertisement

Max opened his wallet for the tenth time, hoping that this time he'd find something there other than a stub from an old movie ticket.

"Totally broke again," moaned Max. "How long is this going to last?" He'd have to come up with something—and soon. If necessary, he could always do without his favorite band's latest CD. But next week his class was going on a field trip, and he wanted to be able to buy at least a soda and something to eat. Besides, he had promised his younger sister, Julia, that he would bring her something.

There was no sense in asking his parents for money. Max had tried that often enough. Ever since his father had lost his job, there wasn't a spare penny to be had in the Hope household.

"I don't see why I should slave away for such silly things," said Mrs. Hope, who worked as a secretary at the high school. In Max's case, the list of silly things seemed endless—going to the movies, buying comics, CDs, and computer games.

For a while Max had earned money by delivering newspapers with his friend Mike. But after their fight, he had lost the job. Officially, you had to be 14 to deliver papers, and Max was just 12. On Sundays, when the newspaper was three times the size of the regular paper, Mike couldn't finish the work by himself, so he asked Max for help. They split the work and the money.

Then two weeks ago, Mike had called Max's friend Sophie stuck-up, and a fight had broken out.

"Take it back," Max demanded.

"I will not!"

"But Sophie is totally not stuck-up. Not at all."

"Oh, so you're in love with her?" Mike had teased, grinning.

"Shut up, don't be stupid. I'm not in love with her!"

"Oh, sure you're not!"

Max was so mad he ran at Mike with fists flying and gave him a bloody lip. Max was glad he had stuck up for Sophie, but it meant he had lost a friend—and a job.

He would just have to look around for another way to earn some money.

With this idea, he picked up the local free newspaper—they no longer had the regular paper delivered—and turned to the tiny Help Wanted section.

*Teacher needed for clarinet lessons.*

"I'm not musical," mumbled Max. And he had never even held a clarinet. Hmmm, too old, too much experience needed, full time, he said to himself as he continued down the short column. Nothing, absolutely nothing! Well, that had been a total waste of time. Now what? "Perhaps a snack would help," he muttered as he moved toward the kitchen. His mother's complaints about "his bottomless pit of a stomach" rang in his head.

While he was making a sandwich, he noticed that his mother had left the latest copy of the high school newspaper lying on the counter. Great, he thought, something to read while I eat. He poured himself some milk, and, with the glass in one hand and the sandwich and paper in the other, he walked over and sat down at the table. His mother was always going on about how hard the students worked on this paper—let's see what's so great about it. He flipped through the pages, reading as he munched till he came to the last page. He was about to toss the whole thing aside when he saw it. A tiny ad in the bottom corner.

*Gardening help needed. Must be fearless and discreet.*

Hmmm, he wondered. Gardening. Cutting the grass and weeding, he could do that. But what did the second part mean? Why would he have to be fearless for gardening work? And discreet?

Maybe he would be burying disgusting things. Or stolen goods. Forbidden and dangerous things. Or even—no! He shook his head. Then the ad would have requested a grave digger, and there was nothing about a cemetery in the description. Maybe the garden was a paradise for flesh-eating plants—incredibly mean, biting things that one could only touch while wearing gloves . . .

Or maybe someone was growing hemp and poppies to make drugs . . . but that was silly. Surely they couldn't

run an ad in the school paper if it was something illegal. Max swallowed hard. He needed a job, and now was the perfect time to make the call. His parents were at a school meeting with his sister. Julia would be starting school in September. She was already excited.

Max punched the number into the phone. It rang and rang. No one home, Max said to himself. Disappointed, he was about to hang up when suddenly someone answered.

"Hammond speaking." It was the broken voice of an old man. He sounded exhausted, as if he had sprinted to the phone.

"Hello, this is Max Hope," said Max, trying to make his voice sound older. "I just read your ad for gardening work. Has the position been filled yet?"

The old man chuckled. "I've had many applicants and just as many rejections." Rejections? This sounded like a demanding job. Max was bursting with curiosity.

"I'm just wondering, why does one have to be fearless?" he asked in a rush.

"Ever had a nightmare?" asked the old man.

"Of course."

"Well, then," was all the old man said.

Max thought for a moment. "And discreet?" he asked. "If this is something illegal, I'm not interested, I just want you to know."

"Discretion serves everyone," said the old man mysteriously. "We can talk about the rest tomorrow. Be here at three o'clock. 29 Juniper Way." The line clicked. The old man had hung up.

Max stared at the receiver. "That guy has a screw loose," he said, shaking his head. "He's lost his marbles. There's something weird about this whole thing." In spite of that, Max had already decided to keep the appointment with the old man. At least it wouldn't cost him anything.

# The 13th Applicant

The next afternoon, Max put on his jacket and made sure that he had his bike lock with him. Juniper Way was way out on the edge of town. Half an hour later he was there. The street was lined with old mansions—some had been renovated, others were pretty dilapidated. Max kept an eye on the addresses. Near the end of the road he found number 27, followed by a tall, wild hedge that looked unending. Max biked alongside it, until Juniper Way ended at the edge of a wooded area. He hadn't found an entrance or a house with the number 29.

Annoyed, Max kept searching. He was out of breath because he had pedaled so fast. He definitely did not want to be late. But it looked as if someone had been pulling his leg.

"Nightmares," he snorted. "I should've known right away that the old man was making it all up."

Slowly, he biked back, angry that he had made the special trip. Just as he passed the middle of the hedge, he braked hard. There was a wrought iron gate with an ornate number 29 on it. On the right side there was even a mailbox.

Shaking his head, Max got off his bike. "I'm sure that

gate wasn't there before. I couldn't have missed it. No way!" he mumbled. He touched the iron bars carefully. They were solid and cold. It wasn't an optical illusion. Max looked at the mailbox. "A. Hammond" was written on the box in a faded, almost illegible script.

There was no bell to be seen. So Max pressed against the gate. It opened with a screech. Behind it began a gravel path, bordered on the left and right by thickly planted fir trees. Max hesitated, then pushed his bike through the gate and up the gravel path. After a short distance, the path made a sharp turn. Max rounded the corner and stopped, surprised.

There, just ahead, stood what seemed to be a little castle. It was surrounded by a wonderful park with flower beds, marble statues, fountains, and ponds. Since it was early spring, not much was in bloom yet, but clumps of snowdrops and purple crocuses gave a hint of how beautiful the park would look later in the year.

"Incredible," mumbled Max. He had never heard anything about this castle or this park, and the Hopes had lived in Tingley for six years.

During the previous school year, Max had gone with his class on a field trip to a big estate where the garden had been the main attraction. Visitors were permitted to look around if they paid the entrance fee. But this castle and its garden didn't appear to be well known. It certainly wasn't on any postcard from Tingley.

And to think that Max might be working here. In the actual garden of what looked like an actual castle!

"Punctual, punctual," said a voice right behind him.

"To be commended."

Max jumped and turned quickly around. There stood an old man. He had snow-white hair and a weathered face that looked as if it had been carved out of wood. Max glanced nervously about. The old man seemed to have appeared out of thin air.

"Hey, pull yourself together," chuckled the old man. "I'm not going to eat you!"

"O-o-of course not," stuttered Max. Then he boldly stretched out his hand. "I'm Max Hope."

"Amadeus Hammond." The man gripped Max's hand and shook it. Max felt how rough and calloused his fingers were. The dark brown eyes scrutinized him from head to toe. They seemed to grasp every detail.

"I had no idea that there was a castle here," said Max. "It's really strange actually, but I could've sworn that there wasn't a gate in the hedge. I couldn't find the entrance until I went back."

He expected an answer like "You have to keep your eyes open!" But instead Hammond replied, "Not every visitor is welcome here. That's why there are certain security measures."

"What kind of security measures?" Max asked curiously.

"You have a password for your computer, don't you? So that no one else can make mischief on it," said Hammond, beckoning for Max to follow him toward the castle.

"Oh, yes," stammered Max, as he stumbled with his bicycle behind the man. It was true. Passwords kept

intruders like moms and sisters from meddling with your private stuff. But a gate was something entirely different from a computer! Max had not seen the gate. And a gate couldn't simply disappear and then suddenly reappear.

"Does the castle belong to you?" Max asked, as he parked his bike in front of the building.

"I am kind of a trustee," Hammond answered. "Trustee and gardener in one. I take care of the park until the legitimate heir appears. But recently there have been a series of crises. Therefore, my application was

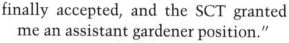

finally accepted, and the SCT granted me an assistant gardener position."

"SCT?" Max repeated.

"The Secret Council of 12," explained Hammond.

That sounded exciting.

"What's that?" Max asked.

"An organization of old and wise men and women." Hammond glanced over his shoulder at Max. "Just call it a club of, uh, garden enthusiasts."

A club of garden enthusiasts. Max was disappointed. That sounded pretty lame. In all likelihood it was a club of plant lovers who funded the park.

"That's why I put the ad in the paper," continued Hammond. "It's not easy to find the right assistant. You are the 13th applicant."

"The 13th?" exclaimed Max.

"Six didn't even get through the gate, another four left on the spot, and the last two didn't pass the test."

"What kind of test?" asked Max, alarmed. "Will I be tested, too?"

"Listen, ever since you've gotten here, you've asked one question after another," answered Hammond brusquely. "My patience is running out. Could you just wait a bit?"

"I'm sorry," mumbled Max.

He followed Hammond up the steps to the entrance.

Along the stone banister stood several large flowerpots with evergreens growing inside them. The evergreens had been trimmed in the shape of animals. Some looked like ducks, others like pigs or snails. It certainly must have been a lot of work to sculpt the bushes so artfully, and even more to keep them that way.

"Anyway, it's just a little aptitude test," said Hammond with a wave of his hand.

"What?" asked Max. He hadn't been listening because he was fascinated by two iron lion heads that hung on the great double doors of the castle.

"The test for the applicants," answered the old man. "Just a tiny, little test, barely even worth mentioning."

As Max continued to stare, the eyes of the lion head on the right seemed to move and look directly at him. The nostrils flared, a light mist rose upward, and the iron ring in its mouth swung back and forth.

Max jerked backward in surprise. He rubbed his eyes and stared at the head again. But now the lion looked as harmless and quiet as the one on the left. Only an object made out of metal, nothing more. Max swallowed. Was he seeing things?

Hammond pressed against the door and stepped into

a large, gloomy hall. A stale odor hung in the air. Max sniffed. It smelled exactly like a museum. As Max's eyes adjusted to the gloom, he saw that the floor was made of shiny black marble. A large red star was set into the floor. Max counted the points.

Five. A pentagram or pentacle. Such a sign was meant to keep away evil spirits. Max had read that in a book about magic in the Middle Ages. But why was it there? Suddenly, the hairs on his arms stood up. He glanced nervously about. From the ceiling of the hall hung a huge chandelier with thousands upon thousands of polished glass pieces.

"Cool lamp," said Max, trying to hide the nervousness in his voice.

"Yes, very valuable," answered Hammond and waved Max to the left of the hallway. There he opened the door to his office. "Come in here."

The room was filled with files and books. In the middle stood a desk that was completely covered with stacks of paper.

"Why do you want the job?" asked Hammond.

"Because I need money." The words just slipped out. Immediately, Max wondered if he should have said something like because I love gardening instead.

"An honest answer." Hammond smiled and sat down at his desk in order to fill out some paperwork. "Your name?"

"Max Hope."

"How old?"

"I'm 12." Max fidgeted as Hammond's eyes bored

into him. Did the old man think that he wasn't old enough for the job? Max was tall and very thin. But he was also very strong. He had inherited his height, dark hair, and brown eyes from his dad. But his stamina and curiosity, his need to look into everything, these things came from his mom.

"Have you ever done garden work before?" Hammond asked.

"Sometimes I help my grandfather. I can cut the grass, I know how to use the pruner, I can weed and spread fertilizer." Max thought a moment. What else had he done? "I have also trimmed roses. Grandfather showed me how to do it. You just have to find where the roses have their eyes . . ."

"Excellent." The old man nodded. "Have you been vaccinated for tetanus?"

"I think so," said Max. "My mother had me vaccinated against everything."

"Well, good." Hammond stood up again. "That's enough for now. The test will show if you are suited for the work. Do you want to start right away?"

"Sure."

"Then come along."

# Not a Job for Weak Nerves

They left the castle through the backdoor. Max would have liked to see some of the rooms concealed behind the many closed doors, but a castle tour was apparently not part of the plan. Hammond led Max to a little brick shed where the garden tools were stored.

"Do you know how to shovel?"

"Of course."

Hammond pointed to an old garden plot and instructed Max to dig. The area was only about three feet square.

"This hasn't been done for years. It's possible that the ground is a little hard. You will need strength and patience," Hammond said.

"No problem," replied Max. He had dug up much bigger areas when working with his grandfather.

"Just throw any rocks you find into the wheelbarrow, and you can dump them behind the shed later."

"Okay," said Max glancing around. "That's it?"

"That's enough for today," said Hammond. "But if you want to, you can cut down those dried-up stalks." He pointed to another plot. Then he showed Max where the pruning shears were and advised him to wear gloves.

"When you're finished, meet me back at my office."
Max nodded, and Hammond disappeared. The boy
started working. He guessed that it would take about
an hour for everything. Enthusiastically, he stuck the
shovel into the dirt. The ground wasn't as hard as he
had feared. Max could easily do this. He whistled
happily to himself and imagined everything he would
do with the money he earned.

The wheelbarrow was filling up quickly. It was as-
tounding to see how many stones were stuck in such
a small area.

Max's grandfather had always claimed that stones
grow in the earth, but Max had never believed him.
Max threw another stone into the wheelbarrow. It
clattered with a satisfying sound when it struck the
metal. But then it skipped out, and Max had to go after

it. As he grabbed the shovel once again, it seemed that the section he had already dug up had become smaller.

"Impossible! That's simply impossible," Max muttered to himself. Vigorously, he started working again. Gradually, he began to sweat and took off his jacket. After a while, he could feel his muscles tiring and could see the first signs of blisters on his hands.

Max had to take a break. He looked at his watch. He had already been shoveling for an hour. And he hadn't finished even a quarter of the little plot!

After that first break, he noticed that he had to stop more and more often. But each time he took a break, it seemed that the section he had just dug up changed back into solid ground.

Finally, Max threw down the shovel angrily. "This is stupid!" He didn't want to finish. Someone was definitely trying to make a fool out of him! But then again, what was happening couldn't *really* be happening. A freshly turned-over piece of ground could not change back into solid ground whenever one turned their back on it. And yet, that was exactly what seemed to be happening.

Max wondered if he should go into the castle and complain. But then he'd lose the job for sure. The old man certainly wouldn't believe a word when he told him what had happened. Max didn't really believe it himself. He stood and scratched his head, wondering what to do.

Dry earth trickled from his fingers. He examined his blisters. It shouldn't be so difficult to dig up this tiny piece of land! Then it occurred to him. "Just a minute," muttered Max to himself. "Whenever I take a break or turn around, the ground becomes hard again. So what happens if I dig without a break?"

He gritted his teeth and grabbed the shovel again. Drops of sweat stood out on his forehead. His arms became heavier and heavier, but he didn't give up. Doggedly, he stuck the shovel into the ground, turned the dirt over, pulled the shovel out, and drove it in again. He pulled the stones out of the ground and threw them over his shoulder, without turning around.

It was working! Soon Max was digging up the last bit of ground. His arms could barely lift the shovel anymore, but he kept going.

"Just . . . one . . . more . . . just . . . one . . . more . . ." Max gasped. The work was almost finished! As the shovel sank into earth one last time, something clinked against the tool. Max bent down and pulled out a round, greenish stone. As he brushed the dirt away, he discovered something carved into the stone.

"Wow!" Max exclaimed. He rubbed the stone against his pants until it started to gleam. He had never seen anything like it before. One side showed a pentagram, the other a four-leaf clover.

Max swallowed hard. Was it a piece of jewelry? The pentagram reminded him of the pentagram in the castle's front hall. A magical symbol? Was the thing supposed to protect against evil spirits? Had he found an old amulet?

For a moment Max had wanted to simply put the

stone in his pocket and take it home. But then he thought it through. The stone belonged to the castle grounds, and Hammond was its supervisor. Max must give the old man what he had found.

He pushed the wheelbarrow to the shed and emptied the stones behind it, like Hammond had told him to. Then he put the shovel back and grabbed the gardening shears and a pair of gloves.

By the time Max finished cutting off all the dried stalks, it was dusk. His back ached as he stood up. A light, hazy mist lay upon the lawn, making the landscape look slightly creepy. But Max discovered upon closer inspection that a few buds were already poking out of the ground.

Exhausted, he put the gardening shears and gloves back, bolted the shed doors, and walked to the castle. Hammond looked up from his desk as Max stepped into the office.

"So, everything taken care of?" he asked.

Max nodded. Then he pulled the green stone out of his jacket pocket and placed it on the table. "I found that while I was digging."

"Oh," said Hammond, looking surprised. He turned the stone over in his hand. "An odd find. A worrystone."

"A worrystone?" repeated Max. "What worries will it save me from?"

"In this world there are more worries than you can imagine, my boy."

Figures, thought Max, just another one of Hammond's puzzling answers. But this time he wanted more. "Are you talking about . . . magic?"

As soon as he said the word *magic*, a stack of books slipped off a shelf in the bookcase behind him and fell to the floor with a crash.

"What was that?" Max cried, whirling around.

"Just a few books," muttered Hammond. As he spoke some pieces of paper fluttered from the desk and sailed onto the floor.

Max's eyes opened wide. "What . . . how did that happen?"

"A draft of wind," answered Hammond quickly. "The windows don't close quite right anymore."

"But it is completely still outside—I didn't feel anything," Max replied. Bewildered, he watched as more papers were lifted from the desk and fluttered through the air.

"It's just one of the quirks in old buildings," explained Hammond. "So many drafts and breezes arise, you know." He bent over the desk in order to hold down the remaining papers. More books fell from another bookcase.

"Stop it!" Hammond said loudly. Everything was still. Carefully, Hammond lifted his arms from the desk and sat back down in his chair. "Now, Max, how did you like the test?" he asked.

Max hesitated. He wasn't sure if it was smart to tell him about the bewitched plot. Maybe he had just imagined the whole thing. Therefore he simply said: "I thought I would have been able to finish it faster."

"And I was convinced that you wouldn't be able to finish it on the first day," retorted the old man. "You have stamina and you *are* smart."

Now Max understood that the garden plot had been his test. He took a step forward. "How did you pull off that trick?"

"What trick?" Hammond looked confused.

"Well, the one with the plot! I want to know how you did it."

"I didn't do anything," Hammond replied coolly. "And you should tame your curiosity a bit."

"So, did I pass the test? Do I get the job?"

Hammond smiled. "You appear to be the right applicant. Otherwise the worrystone wouldn't have found you."

Max was pleased with the praise, but he was confused, too. Hammond had such a strange way of expressing himself.

"You mean, otherwise I wouldn't have found the worrystone," Max said.

"No," replied Hammond, "worrystones search for those who are supposed to find them. And therefore the stone belongs to you." He pushed the green stone across the table toward Max. "Take good care of it."

"Thanks." Max was still a bit confused, but he happily stuck the stone into his pocket.

"Can you come again tomorrow?" asked Hammond. "Let's say, again around three?"

"Yup."

"Good. Then, see you tomorrow," Hammond said,

turning his attention back to his desk.

Max understood that he had been dismissed, but he didn't want to go before he knew how much he would be getting paid.

"Is there something else?" Hammond looked up again.

"Uh—my wages?" Max asked in a tentative voice.

"I will write down your hours, and at the end of the week everything will be tallied up. This will be your hourly rate." He slid a slip of paper with something scribbled on it toward Max. "How is that?"

Max nodded, pleased with the amount. He was about to turn to go when suddenly something banged on the

desk. Then a few pieces of paper fluttered into the air and Hammond jerked them back into place.

Max watched in fascination as Hammond quickly brushed the air above his shoulder as if something had just landed there. But when the old man noticed that the boy was watching, he tried to make the movement into a harmless gesture.

"A fly—just a troublesome fly."

Max was 100 percent certain that there was not a single fly in the room. He didn't know what was going on, but he had a very strong feeling that there was definitely something peculiar about the whole thing.

"Well, then, good-bye," said Hammond, forcing a smile.

"Good-bye," repeated Max in a weak voice. He quickly left the room and pulled the door closed behind him. His stomach had turned to knots and his heart was racing. Was he going crazy?

Then he heard Hammond's voice from behind the door, speaking in the same harsh tone he had used before, "That's enough, Nepomuk!"

Max took a deep breath. Who was Hammond talking to? No one else had been in the room. And who, or what, had thrown the books from the bookshelves? What had played with all the papers on the desk?

And what could have possibly jumped onto Hammond's shoulder? Max was tempted to open the door once more. His hand was already reaching for the doorknob. But a loud crash stopped him cold.

*Crash!*

It sounded like someone—or *something*—was making a mess of Hammond's office.

*Crash!*

"Hammond? Are you okay?" Max shouted. There was no answer, and, as the crashes grew louder, he turned and ran as fast as he could down the hallway toward the exit.

# A Confidential Conversation

Shortly afterward, Hammond placed a phone call from the castle.

*"You're saying he passed the test?"*

"Just a little Level Two endurance test. He is only 12."

*"Only 12? He is still just a child! Have you gone crazy, Hammond?"*

"He made a brilliant impression on me."

*"Brilliant? What good does that do us? You know what characteristics your candidate must have, they must be absolutely fearless . . ."*

"Yes, I know, and discreet. My memory still works."

*"Don't get sassy, Hammond."*

"I would ask you to do the same."

*"Do you even know what sort of responsibilities you are carrying?"*

"Yes, I know them quite well. And I am overwhelmed. I want to hand over my job, finally. But this heir is still missing and isn't taking care of his inheritance."

*"We think he may be in America."*

"Well, he is not here, and I am tired of it. Initially, I was nothing more than the gardener. Planting, picking, repotting—I know how to do those sorts of things. I like to watch the plants as they grow, and I am happy when they thrive. But in hindsight I never would have agreed to what I do now."

*"Think about your promise!"*

"I don't think about anything else. And I bitterly regret that I made that promise. But one will promise anything to a man on his deathbed. 'You have to help me, Hammond, you are my only support.' And then his feverish look and his closed eyes. 'Take care of my creatures. Care for them well.' And like an idiot I said 'Yes' just so he could finally die in peace."

*"Right. You agreed to his request."*

"And I bemoan that decision. I have hardly slept in the last few days. The creatures in Department Four are becoming more and more restless. They are practically

ready to rebel. I don't know how long I can hold them at bay. I just can't allow myself to lose anymore time. I need support, otherwise I can't continue. Therefore, I am happy that the boy came."

*"But he is just a child! Children are curious, they stick their noses into everything, they never keep their mouths shut, they shirk responsibility . . ."*

"This boy is different."

*"I hope you haven't made a mistake, Hammond. You can be sure that the Secret Council of 12 will be involved with this matter. If one of the creatures gets away, there will be disastrous consequences. And then you will be held responsible, Hammond!"*

# The Power of the Worrystone

*Meep-meep-meep-meep.*

Max pushed the snooze button on his alarm clock. He had been dreaming that he was running through a big labyrinth. In the middle, a bright red chinchilla had hopped up to him, jumped onto his shoulder, and squeaked into his ear, "I am Nepomeep-meep-meep."

Somewhat dazed, Max got out of bed and shuffled to the bathroom. At breakfast he was so quiet that his dad asked what was wrong with him.

"Nothing," mumbled Max. "I just don't want to talk right now. You know the feeling, right?"

His mom smiled. "My two lovely morning grumps," she said tenderly. "But tomorrow is Saturday, you can sleep in." She never had a problem waking up in the mornings. Julia was the same way. She could get up at six and talk up a storm. But dad needed his coffee first, and Max was rarely very talkative before eight.

That's why he wasn't happy when his friend Sophie pounced on him as soon as he stepped inside the classroom. She even sat on his desk, so he couldn't unpack his stuff.

"How's it going?" she asked cheerfully, pulling her blonde hair into a ponytail.

"Good. I got a job," answered Max. Since Sophie didn't make a move, he carefully put his pencils down next to her and laid his ruler on top.

"What kind of job?"

"Garden work." Max turned his hands over so that she could see the blisters. "I really slaved away yesterday, and today I'm going back."

"And how much are you getting for it?"

"It's good money for gardening," said Max.

"Hmmm," said Sophie. Then she leaned forward. "Can you explain the math homework to me this afternoon? If we have a test next week, I'm dead. I haven't understood anything. Nada."

Max thought about it. "I only have an hour. You'd have to come right after school."

"Okay." Sophie slid from the desk just as the bell rang.

Mrs. Greary, the geography teacher, was the epitome of punctuality. And today was no exception. With her customary military stride, she came into the classroom and heaved her book onto the lectern. "Good morning. Is everyone here, is anyone absent? Remove your books and notebooks from your desks. I hope everyone is prepared for a test."

Oh no! thought Max. He had completely forgotten there would be a test today. He hadn't even studied. And the questions were hard. He knew he would surely get a big fat **F**! Max could already see his mother's face.

Suddenly, he felt something hard pressing against his thigh. Max stuck his left hand into his pants' pocket and touched the worrystone. At that very moment, a balled-up note landed on his desk. Quick as lightning, Max covered it with his free hand. He had never cheated on a test before. Maybe the note had landed inadvertently on his desk. His heart was racing as he carefully flattened out the paper. Mrs. Greary was looking out the window.

The right answers! Max's hand shook as he filled out the test. He expected that at any moment he would be caught red-handed and thunder would clap over his head. After he had written down the answers, he crumpled the paper again and slipped it into his pocket. Then Mrs. Greary turned back around.

"Put your pencils down. Pass your papers forward."

It was Sophie and Jonas's turn to help. As Sophie passed by Max, she winked at him. Now Max knew who the cheat sheet was from. Mrs. Greary stowed the tests in her black bag and started the daily lesson.

Max wanted to thank Sophie during the break between classes, but she was with two other girls the whole time and after school she disappeared immediately.

# Sophie Doesn't Give Up

Max had not been home long, however, when Sophie rang the Hopes' doorbell. Max's mother opened it. "Hello, Sophie." She smiled. "We met before, at the school's Christmas party. You were the angel."

"Oh, right." Sophie grimaced. "Max and I were the only ones from our class who volunteered for the manger scene. Everyone else still makes fun of us. Is Max home?"

"He's eating, as usual! Would you like some raspberry pudding, too?"

"No, thanks."

Max appeared in the kitchen doorway.

"Hi, Sophie." He was wiping crumbs from his mouth. "We're going to my room to study, Mom."

Sophie followed him down the hall and surveyed his room. "Nice," she said.

"It's not exactly clean at the moment," apologized Max. "And it's definitely not as nice as your house." Sophie's parents were dentists and had a huge house with a gigantic garden.

"How would you know? You've never been over." Sophie sat down on Max's bed, because his clothes covered the chair. "Actually why haven't you ever come over to my house?"

Max tried to skirt the question, but Sophie was staring at him. "Well, ummm, then it would seem, uh, like we were going out or something."

Sophie shrugged. "You know, my mother always says, let other people say what they want." But she changed the subject. "Anyway, I'm interested in your job. Do you need any help? I like plants. My mother always says I have a green thumb." Her blue eyes sparkled.

Max hesitated. "The job is actually a little bit weird," he finally said, and then he began to tell her what had happened the day before.

"I have never heard of a castle or a park on Juniper before," Sophie exclaimed excitedly. "And a gate that can disappear—how bizarre!"

"I've even thought that maybe the Secret Council is behind everything. The Secret Council of 12 . . ." Max said ominously.

"Stop exaggerating." Sophie giggled. "You've seen too many movies."

Max stuck his hand in his pocket and pulled out the worrystone. "And look what I found yesterday while digging."

Sophie bent over the stone. "Oh, that's fantastic." She was really impressed.

"Hammond called it a worrystone," explained Max. "I'm not usually superstitious, but today in geography, I was panicking about the test, and suddenly I remembered that I had this thing, and then your note came."

Sophie's forehead wrinkled.

"Anyway, thanks again," said Max. "I would've totally failed without your help."

"No problem. You help me with math all the time." Sophie carefully tapped the stone. "So, just because I helped you, now you think this thing has special powers?"

Max shrugged his shoulders. "I dunno."

"I'd really like to see that park," Sophie announced. "Can I go with you later?"

Max thought about it. "Okay," he said finally. "Then you can see it yourself and tell me if my brain is working right or if I'm just imagining all this stuff. But for now let's work on your math."

Sophie grinned. "Could you lend me the worrystone for the next math test?"

"Don't you believe me?"

"Not everything, Mr. Vivid Imagination!"

# The Open Door

"You should be a math teacher," said Sophie, as Max shut the book. "I understand it when you explain it. Anyway, Mr. Kern can't stand me."

The math teacher did seem to take pleasure in calling Sophie to the board and making her do problems in front of the entire class. If she did something wrong or hesitated even a bit, he made remarks. Sophie, who wasn't used to holding her tongue, often defended herself with quick-witted responses. The entire class was amused by the exchanges. But when it came to Sophie's math grade, the situation was not so amusing.

"At least I have a better grasp of the math homework for next week," said Sophie.

Max glanced at his watch. "We've gotta go," he said and quickly packed his math book into his backpack. In the hallway they put their jackets on.

"I'm going to Sophie's house," he said to his mother.

"Okay," replied Mrs. Hope. "But don't be late. You know when dinnertime is."

"When are you actually going to tell your parents that you have a job?" asked Sophie, as they went down the stairs together. "You can't keep it a secret forever."

"I have to wait for the right moment. My mom will

worry that it will hurt my schoolwork."

They reached the bottom of the stairs at the same time. As Max went to the garage, Sophie unlocked her bike and waited until Max brought out his bike.

"Let's go," said Max, and swung his leg over the seat.

"Can't wait," answered Sophie and pedaled behind him.

Out of breath, they finally reached Juniper Way. Sophie barely glanced at the old houses. Finally they came to the hedge. It looked impenetrable. No one would ever guess that behind it lay a well-maintained castle and grounds. At best it looked like there might be a dilapidated house and overgrown garden. Then the gate in the hedge appeared. Max braked. "We're here."

Sophie jumped off her bike. "Hard to find, eh?" she mocked.

"I swear to you, Sophie, yesterday the gate wasn't there right away," answered Max. "I have no idea how this works—but Hammond can somehow make it appear and then disappear . . ."

"What, with magic? Hocus-pocus disappearus?"

"I don't know," replied Max. "Maybe there's some sort of mechanism."

"It doesn't matter. Let's go in." Sophie opened the gate; today it squeaked quietly on its hinges. The gravel path crunched beneath their tires as they pushed the bikes down the path. After a while the fir trees were behind them and they had a clear view of the castle and park.

Sophie stood in awe. "It's incredible! Wow, it is so

43

pretty here!" she exclaimed.

Max led the way down the path toward the castle, and they leaned their bikes against the steps to the front door. "Hammond is probably in his office." Max turned around. "Would you mind waiting outside? I want to ask Hammond first if you can work with me."

Sophie shrugged her shoulders. "If that's better, sure."

"I'll be right back," promised Max.

Sophie sat down on the stoop. The sun crept out from between the clouds. The smell of spring hung in the air. Sophie let her eyes wander over the park. All over the lawn the crocuses were blooming—orange, purple, white. Sophie was thinking it would be marvelous to live here, to have the entire park at your disposal, to go for a walk whenever your heart desired.

She looked at the evergreens planted in big flowerpots on her left and right along the stairs. She thought it was funny how the plants were cut into animal shapes. She especially liked the ducks. It would be even funnier if the ducks were looking at one another. Sophie stood and turned the right flowerpot until the duck's beak pointed inward. The pot was heavier than she had expected. It took a lot of effort to move it. But finally the duck stood just as she had imagined. "And now for the other one . . ."

She started working on the left pot. It was even heavier, but finally the ducks were looking at each other. "Much better." Sophie wiped her hands on her jeans and sat back down on the steps. When she raised her eyes, she stared in disbelief. The duck on the left was moving! It stretched its neck, bent forward, and hopped out of the pot. Sophie stood and stared. She could not believe what she was seeing. The duck waddled toward the middle of the step, stood still, and let out a challenging *quack, quack!* Sophie's hands flew to her mouth. Then the duck on the right came to life. It hopped out of the pot and waddled toward the other duck. Then both ducks started to twitch. The evergreen branches were melting into one another. Little leaves trickled to the ground.

"I've gone crazy," whispered Sophie. "I'm hallucinating. Oh, no!"

Both of the ducks were strangely illuminated. They lost their duck shape and merged first into one shimmering ball and then into one human-sized figure. Sophie gasped. Before her stood a woman in a green robe. The robe was covered with golden sequins that sparkled in the sun. The woman brushed her long blonde hair back from her face and smiled at Sophie.

"Hello!" she said.

"Wh . . . wh . . . who are you?" asked Sophie. Her teeth chattered as she spoke.

"Thank you for freeing me," said the stranger with the friendliest voice that Sophie had ever heard. "I wish to reward you with gold."

"Fr-fr-freeing?" stuttered Sophie.

"Yes, thank you," repeated the woman reaching her hand toward Sophie. "I'm going to give you gold. A lot of gold. You have to come with me." Sophie jerked away from her hand and looked at the stranger fearfully.

"The gold lies at the bottom of the pond," said the woman with a tempting tone in her voice. "It's easy to pull it out. Then you will be rich. You want to be rich, don't you?"

Sophie shook her head hard. "N-n-n-ooo! NO!

Absolutely not! I want—HELP!" Heart pounding, Sophie turned and raced up the steps. She could hear the woman laughing behind her. With all her might, Sophie pushed the heavy doors open and burst into the entrance hall.

# Witch's Gold

"Max. MAAAX!" Sophie's voice echoed from the vaulted ceiling. At the end of the walkway, Max stepped out of a door, accompanied by Hammond. Sophie threw herself at them and grabbed onto Max's arm. "Out-outside, there is a gh-ghost. A wi-witch. I don't know." Her sentences were getting tangled. "I-I freed her, I think, but I on-only turned the fl-flowerpots and then the ducks . . ." She had to take a deep breath.

"Slow down! I can't understand a word you're saying," said Max. A noise came from the entrance. Sophie turned around. The doors had opened. The woman stepped into the hall.

"There she is," whispered Sophie.

Hammond let out a scream. He turned toward the wall.

"Whatever you do, don't look at her! Close your eyes!" He covered his face and moaned. Then he mumbled the words, "*Quieta nonmovere!*" It sounded like a spell.

"Too late," responded the woman. "Free is free." And her laughter floated toward them from across the hall. Sophie glanced over her shoulder. She couldn't take her eyes off the woman.

The stranger crossed the hall. Suddenly she stopped and hesitated. She stared down at the pentagram and quickly pulled her foot back. Then she looked up, directly at Sophie's face. Her green eyes sparkled. "A thousand thanks for my freedom!" she called tauntingly and beckoned with her hand. "I will make you rich. Come and get the golden treasure. Then you can buy anything you desire."

Hammond let out a loud groan. "Don't believe it," he mumbled without turning around. "It's just an evil trick!"

Neither Max nor Sophie even heard his warning. They were already mesmerized by the woman and her green cloak, which shimmered and glowed in the lamplight.

"Come get your treasure," repeated the stranger in a sly voice.

"I don't want it," exclaimed Sophie, as she hid behind Max. She wouldn't trust that woman for all the gold in the world! The stranger shook her head, as if she couldn't understand Sophie's words. Then she moved her eyes to Max.

"Is that girl your friend?" she asked coyly.

Max nodded.

"Then I will give the gold to you," the woman purred.

"You can buy something pretty for her."

"Ahh . . . hmm . . ." Max seemed to be trying to clear his throat.

"Come and get it," the woman continued. "The gold is outside in the pond. It is very easy to find."

"Very easy," said Max in a weak voice and took a small step forward.

"No!" Sophie held onto his arm tightly. "We don't need the gold." Max freed himself of her grip and actually shoved Sophie aside.

"Hey, what was that for?" asked Sophie angrily.

"Gold," cooed the woman and pointed at Max with her finger.

"Gold," repeated Max, as if hypnotized.

"Then come, my boy," murmured the stranger.

Sophie watched in horror as Max went forward. He appeared to have forgotten everything else and moved like a zombie toward the woman. "Max!" she shouted. "Stop! STOP! She's put a spell on you!"

Max didn't seem to hear. Sophie looked pleadingly at Hammond, who was still leaning against the wall, his hands pressed against his face. "Do something!" she yelled.

"*Remaneo vacuus aqua,*" Hammond stammered.

"I don't understand Latin!" Sophie angrily replied.

"Too late! Your young friend—all is lost."

Sophie let out a scream and ran to catch up with Max. She tried to grab hold of him and rooted her feet to the floor. "Don't go with her, Max!" She pulled with all her might. "Don't follow her!"

50

But Max hurled Sophie out of his way with so much force that she fell and slid along the floor. Then he stepped through the entrance with the witch and the doors closed behind them with a loud crack.

Sophie sat in the middle of the pentagram, shaking with anger and disbelief.

"Is she gone?" The question came from Hammond. He had turned away from the wall and was peering at Sophie through his fingers. "She's gone," he answered the question himself, letting his hands fall and looking quite relieved.

Sophie wanted to slap him. What a weakling! He had simply closed his eyes while her friend was led away by that witch!

"Do something!" Sophie cried. Then she flung herself against the doors and ran outside. In the distance, she saw Max and the witch walking together down the path. Sophie raced toward them, wondering how she could free Max from the cruel spell.

"Wait!" she yelled. "Stop! Come back! Maaaaax!"

He didn't seem to hear her, but soon he and the witch slowed down, then stopped alongside a pond and started walking toward the water's edge.

"There lies the treasure," said the witch to Max, pointing. "You have to dive down and bring it up; then it will belong to you."

Max moved like a sleepwalker toward the pond. He appeared to have forgotten that it was still early March and the water would be freezing.

With a loud cry, Sophie reached Max, seized his arm,

and pulled him away from the edge of the pond. "Are you crazy? You'll catch your death!" she screamed.

The woman laughed. "Don't bother, my dear. He can't hear you. Now he belongs to me, only to me!"

"We'll see about that," hissed Sophie. "If you don't leave Max alone, you'll have to go back to being a tree duck. Go back to your flowerpot, you belong there!"

"Ha-ha!" The witch bent her head back, laughing. "But you freed me! Thank you very, very much!"

Sophie was so angry that she grabbed onto a broken branch, wanting to hurl it at the witch. But like lightning an idea came to her. She remembered how the witch had hesitated in the entrance hall.

The pentagram! The magical sign!

Quickly Sophie began to draw a five-sided star with the branch in the mud on the edge of the pond. She wasn't used to drawing such signs and the star was bent and crooked. Still it was a pentagram. She pushed Max into the safety of the middle.

"Clever, clever," jeered the woman. "Do you really think that with this little symbol you can break the power of the gold?" But Sophie could tell that she was

angry.The woman stroked her long blonde hair until it shone and glinted in the sun like gold. Then she slowly slid into the pond. The icy water didn't seem to bother her. She turned onto her back and swam a few strokes, as if it were the middle of summer. Then she turned back to Sophie and Max.

"Come now, my young friend," she called temptingly. Her voice sounded like music. "The water is wonderful."

"I have to go to her," mumbled Max.

"You don't have to do anything!" snorted Sophie. "She's bewitched you! Can't you tell?" Desperately, she wondered how she could bring Max to his senses again.

"Come, my friend," cooed the woman again, impatience creeping into her voice. "The gold will give you power. The future lies in your hands."

Max again tried to tear himself away from Sophie. He almost succeeded in leaving the protection of the pentagram. But Sophie pulled him with so much force that they both fell over. They wrestled with each other. Sophie felt the cold mud on her back. Finally she sat right on top of him and looked down into his face. His eyes were still totally distant. Sophie wondered what else she could possibly do. Then she leaned down and pressed her hands over Max's ears.

He grabbed onto her wrists, trying to pull her hands away. But after a moment his strength failed. His face relaxed. For a brief moment his eyes were clear. He looked at Sophie and seemed to recognize her.

Then his mouth contorted, his eyes rolled back into

his head, and closed.

"MAX!" He was unconscious. Sophie groaned and got up. She took his feet and raised them, so that the blood would rush to his head. They had been taught to do this in health class when someone became unconscious. Frantically, she tapped his cheeks and called his name. "Max! You have to wake up, Max!" she cried, but Max did not wake up. In a total panic she knelt over him. Maybe mouth-to-mouth resuscitation would help. She had seen it done on TV. Gently, she touched his lips with her own. His lips were cool. Sophie tried to blow

into them, but she wasn't sure what else to do. Then it became a kiss. Confused, Sophie sat up and pulled her hair back.

"Hey," Max said, "what's going on?" He was staring at her and his gaze was clear and natural once more.

Sophie felt her face turning red. Had he noticed the kiss? She hesitated for a minute. "Come on, stand up," she said tentatively, still not sure if the spell was really broken.

"Why are we here at the pond's edge?" asked Max gazing around. He didn't seem to remember anything. Then he noticed his clothes. "*Iiiick*, we look like pigs. Totally covered with mud."

"I'll explain it to you later," said Sophie in a rush.

It was too dangerous there at the water's edge. Who could guarantee that the witch wouldn't try a second time? Sophie would've rather gone straight home and forgotten about this bewitched castle. But she had too

many questions. What was going on here anyway? What did Hammond have to do with everything? Now Sophie didn't doubt for a moment what Max had said about his experiences from the previous day. There was definitely something creepy about this park!

"We have to go back to the castle," she said to Max.

While they were walking she kept glancing over her

shoulder at the pond. The woman had disappeared. Only a stone dolphin stuck out of the water. It looked as if it had been frozen mid-jump. After a moment, Sophie heard a quiet splashing. Immediately, goose-bumps covered her arms and she grabbed Max and pulled him forward.

"Come on, let's go!" she cried.

"Why are you in such a hurry?" asked Max, stumbling behind her.

"Oh Max, don't you remember anything?"

But he only shook his head. Sophie briefly described what had happened and how she had been able to rescue him only with great effort. Max was horrified. "The witch wanted to tempt me into the water? She wanted to drown me?" he asked in disbelief.

Sophie nodded. "I'm afraid so." They stared at each other. It seemed as if they had gotten themselves mixed up in something from which there was no turning back. Max was completely confused. He couldn't understand why Hammond hadn't intervened. Whose side was he on? Despite the strange things that had happened the day before, Max had trusted him. He had taken him for someone who knew all the answers and could give advice and help.

"If I had known, I never would have taken this job!" Max exclaimed. "And we would've been spared this whole mess."

"Too late," said Sophie.

"But what now?"

"We'll just have to ask Hammond."

# The Hunt for Mafalda

Hammond was sitting in his office, his hands covering his face. As Sophie and Max stepped into the room, he lifted his head and looked at Max as if he had been raised from the dead.

"You're still alive?" he asked feebly.

"Would you rather I were dead?" Max shouted. What a coward! Max couldn't believe Hammond had just left them to their fate.

"So, who's the water witch?" asked Sophie. She was pacing with anger and impatience. She felt like grabbing Hammond by the shoulders and shaking him. Once and for all, she wanted to know what was going on here. "What does she want? Where is she from?" She squinted at the old man with narrowed eyes.

"She's not a witch," sighed Hammond. "She is a river specter."

"A river specter?" repeated Sophie.

"The water is her element," explained Hammond. "You know, like mermaids, nymphs, sirens . . ."

"Fairy tale characters," sniffed Sophie, still not quite believing.

"Didn't you know how dangerous she was?" asked Max.

Hammond groaned. "Of course. Don't you understand anything? Water specters are tremendously evil and cruel." He paused, as if just forming the words took tremendous effort. "They bring men to ruin. In the spring they are the most dangerous. Horrible creatures! Completely dreadful, even if they are beautiful. As soon as a man looks at a river specter, all is lost. Without hope. She tempts and lures him into the water, coaxing him to get the treasure. And then he drowns." He looked at Max and Sophie, as if he were asking for their understanding. "That's why I couldn't help you before. She would've bewitched me in exactly the same way and I would've followed her into the water."

Max and Sophie exchanged a look, unsure if they should take his explanation for an apology. Hammond stood and went to Sophie. "Tell me, how did you rescue him? Normally it is impossible!" he cried, grabbing her wrists.

Sophie pulled away in surprise. She wasn't sure if she should trust Hammond. She was still mad at him.

"What did you do?" Hammond repeated. "Every detail is important. Maybe we have a chance to stop her."

His voice sounded urgent, so Sophie tried to remember. Only now that everything was over did she realize how much she had done.

"I drew a pentagram in the mud . . ."

"Ingenious!" cried Hammond.

". . . and I put Max in the middle. Then I held my hands over his ears."

"Brilliant!" Hammond clapped his hands.

"I guess since Max couldn't hear, the spell was broken," said Sophie timidly. But then something else occurred to her. "Also Max had the worrystone with him."

Max felt in his pants' pocket and brought the worrystone out. "There it is." The green stone lay shimmering in his hand.

"The stone, of course." Hammond cleared his throat. "The stone surely protected you. But this girl here, this Sarah—"

"Sophie," corrected Sophie.

"Sophie, yes, she saved your life, Max."

Max turned to Sophie and smiled. "Thanks," he said.

Sophie blushed and looked away, embarrassed.

"This girl has a lot of talent," continued Hammond. "I would even go so far as to say that she has magical potential . . ."

"Me and magic?" Sophie shook her head. The thought was completely crazy. "No way."

"Now we have to think about how we're going to capture the river specter again," said Hammond, his

brow wrinkling. "Otherwise she'll just do more damage. Not to mention what would happen if she left the park. Where is she?"

"The last I saw, she was in the dolphin pond," recalled Sophie. She grew nervous as Hammond's eyes rested on her.

"You will have to do it," he said.

Sophie wasn't surprised. Why hadn't she just gone home when she had the chance? For that matter, why had she come at all?

"You can do it. You can tempt her back," Hammond urged. "As a girl you are in less danger than Max and I. You don't have to cover your eyes."

"But I . . ." Sophie tried to protest, but Hammond had already twirled around and was heading toward the wall.

Now Sophie and Max saw the wall safe. The old man quickly spun the dial, first one way, then the other. It clicked a few times; then the door sprang open. Hammond stuck his hands into the opening and pulled out a treasure chest that was covered with dark red velvet. He closed the door to the safe and set the chest on his desk.

"This is the bait for the river specter," he said, opening the lid. Sophie let out a gasp. On a velvet pillow sparkled a golden necklace, covered with shimmering stones. It was unbelievably beautiful. Normally, Sophie didn't think much of jewelry, but this looked as if it were meant for a queen. Sophie had a strong urge to try it on right away and gaze at herself in the mirror.

"There is nothing that river specters like more than gold," explained Hammond. "Gold, gold, gold— that's what they desire the most. With that necklace, you have to lure the river specter back to the steps—exactly to the spot where she first appeared. Max and I will take care of the rest."

With trembling fingers, Sophie caressed the necklace and took it carefully out of the chest. The gold felt heavy in her hands. Now she could see that it was decorated with tiny golden shells and fishes.

"How beautiful!" she whispered.

"Show her the necklace. But under no circumstances are you to give it to her," warned Hammond. "Every ounce of gold increases her power."

Sophie nodded. Her stomach had twisted into knots.

Hammond leaned toward her. "She is called Mafalda," he whispered, as if he didn't trust himself to say the name out loud. "But don't say it more than three times, otherwise it will lose its effectiveness. Now hurry. If the river specter gets away and leaves the park, it will be a catastrophe. Not to mention what she could do to Tingley. We can't waste any time."

Sophie closed her fingers around the necklace.

"Would it be better if I came with you?" asked Max, looking worried.

Hammond shook his head. "Too risky. She has to do it alone. Our task is to catch her again."

Sophie would've liked to have Max by her side, but she also remembered how helpless he had been under Mafalda's influence. She didn't want to experience that again. "Everything will be fine," she said, trying to sound confident and sure. "See you later." She gave Max a bright smile and went to the door.

"Good luck," said Max weakly.

"Knock on wood!" called Hammond after her.

Sophie quickly left the office, ran down the corridor, and crossed over the pentagram in the entrance hall. The doors were heavy. They slipped from her hands and closed with a crash behind her. At first Sophie was blinded by the sun. The sight of the empty flowerpots sent a shiver down her spine. She still wasn't sure if she believed in all this magic and things. But she had seen how the river specter had appeared out of thin air. What sort of laws ruled this park? How could reality have so little power here?

But there was no time for pondering. Determined, Sophie hurried down the steps. She would just have to lure the river specter out of the water. As she ran down the path, she could feel her heart pounding against her ribs. By the time she reached the dolphin pond, her side was aching. She squinted, but she couldn't see the river specter anywhere. The surface of the water was completely smooth. Far to the left, a lone duck paddled, making little waves.

Sophie bit her lip. Had Mafalda already left the park and gone into town? Doubtfully, she gazed at the sparkling necklace in her hand. Was the bait useless now? No, it couldn't be! Sophie took a deep breath and yelled in a commanding voice: "Mafalda!"

Immediately, she could feel the magical power of the name. The air seemed to vibrate. The birds stopped singing, and for a single moment, it was quiet as the grave.

Something splashed in the pond right beside her, and she jumped. Mafalda's head rose out of the water. Her long hair dragged like seaweed behind her.

"Who calls me?" she asked in a light voice.

Sophie felt her knees go weak with surprise. She hadn't expected that Mafalda would appear so quickly. Or that she would be so close. Sophie gathered her courage.

"I did," she answered boldly and moved her hand so that the golden jewel glinted in the sun. "Look what I have!"

Mafalda's expression changed instantly. Her smile vanished and her eyes filled with greed. In a flash, the river specter straightened up, bringing herself halfway out of the water.

"Mine!" croaked Mafalda, longingly stretching out her arms. Sophie gazed at the white hands with the long green fingernails. The word claws shot through her head, and she took a step back.

"Yes, the gold is for you," said Sophie, trying to keep

her voice from trembling.

"Give it to me!"

"You have to come and get it." Sophie took another step. She didn't know how fast Mafalda was or what kind of powers she possessed. Better safe than sorry. If the river specter simply jumped out of the water and ripped the necklace from her hand, then all would be lost!

Mafalda moved toward the pond's edge. She didn't let the gold out of her sight and followed Sophie's every movement. Sophie kept moving backward. Although the distance between herself and Mafalda was still great, she had an uneasy feeling. Would she be able to make it back to the steps? All at once, the castle seemed to be awfully far away.

"Wait for me," called Mafalda.

"I am," Sophie replied, though she took another small step away from the pond.

The river specter stopped. "I don't like this game," she cried, pouting. "You're just teasing me."

Sophie was not sure what to do next. It was clear she had to think of something new or else Mafalda would lose her desire for the gold.

"Don't be silly," said Sophie. "Just come here and get it. Look at how nicely it shines in the sun." She held the necklace out and the gold sparkled enticingly.

Mafalda hesitated, then stepped toward Sophie. Sophie waited. Her heart was pounding. She shouldn't let Mafalda get too close.

The river specter stopped again, as if she knew what

Sophie was thinking.

"What if you are trying to capture me," mused Mafalda. "That's a possibility."

Sophie's heart sank. "Whatever," she said, trying to sound ambivalent. "The necklace is a gift. Because you love gold so much."

Mafalda crossed her arms over her chest. "I have enough already."

"But surely you don't have such a magnificent necklace! Look—it looks like it was made for a queen." Sophie held the necklace up to her own neck.

Mafalda still hesitated, and so Sophie decided to use, for the second time, the powerful name.

"Come on, Mafalda," she said temptingly. "Come and get the gold!"

Mafalda's greed overtook her and she glided forward. Sophie took a step toward the specter, but then stepped back again, carefully as before, step by step. What would she do if Mafalda lost her desire for the gold again? She was only allowed to use her name once more, but would that be enough? Would she reach the steps?

"Stand still!" commanded the river specter after a few feet.

Sophie knew this was never going to work. She had to change her tactic.

"Actually, I think I would rather keep the necklace," said Sophie, suddenly. "It's really quite pretty. And it looks great on me. Why should I give it to you?" With shaking fingers she put the necklace around her own throat and closed the clasp.

Mafalda's face contorted with anger. "You want to take away my gold?" she cried.

"My gold, my gold," Sophie mimicked the river specter. "I like the necklace, and it belongs to me, so that's that!"

Mafalda hissed and stumbled toward Sophie with an outstretched arm. Sophie turned and took off as fast as she could. She could hear Mafalda gasping behind her. The river specter was right on her heels!

Sophie had won. The trick had worked. But Mafalda was incredibly fast! Sophie could almost feel her breath on her neck. And were her fingernails already scratching at her jacket?

Sophie ran for her life. She could not even risk looking back.

"Give . . . it . . . here!" gasped Mafalda, her voice at Sophie's ear. Fifty feet. Forty. Sophie felt fingers on her neck, grabbing at the necklace, then slipping away. She felt her strength ebbing, yet she kept running. Just

twenty feet. Ten. The first step.

Suddenly, she was jerked back. Mafalda had grabbed hold of the necklace and held it tight, strangling Sophie, so that she couldn't breathe.

"Mine," gasped Mafalda, pulling harder. Black dots began to dance in front of Sophie's eyes.

* * * GP * * *

Max looked nervously toward the door. He didn't like it at all that Sophie had gone to search for the witch all by herself. He decided to go against Hammond's decision and stood up from his chair.

"I have to help her!"

"Then you might as well write your will, silly boy," sighed Hammond. "You won't have as much luck the second time!"

Max hesitated. He didn't have any reasonable explanation for everything that had happened, but it was

clear he had barely escaped death the last time he had come in contact with the river specter.

Hammond watched him and nodded. "You are reasonable. Good." He pulled a drawer open and took out a pair of sunglasses. "Here, these are for you." He shoved the glasses across the table. Then he dug further into the drawer and brought out a second pair of glasses. Tentatively, Max put the sunglasses on.

"Do they fit?" asked Hammond. "Otherwise we can switch." The glasses were a little too big and were crooked.

"What do we need the glasses for?" Max asked, pushing the glasses up toward his forehead, so he could see better.

"They will protect our eyes from Mafalda's gaze," explained Hammond. "They are special glasses with a magic filter."

Max stared at the old man. When this was over, Hammond had a lot of explaining to do. It's not like they lived in the Middle Ages, where everyone still believed in magic and witches! After all, this was the 21st century!

Hammond opened a small tin box and handed something to Max.

"Earplugs. What for?"

"So we can't hear Mafalda's tempting song," answered Hammond.

"Are they endowed with magic filters, too?" Max asked in a mocking tone.

"No, they're from the drugstore," replied Hammond

and stood up. "If the ears are plugged, no magic is possible." He poked a finger into Max's chest. "Now do you believe that river specters are highly dangerous? Normal locks and confinements are useless. They need a magical cage and a strong magic spell."

"What is going on here?" Max pushed Hammond's finger away. "This isn't normal at all! Magic! Spells!

River specters! Am I in some kind of ghost park or something?"

"I guess you could call it that."

"WHAT?" Max exclaimed.

"I'll explain later," Hammond sighed. "Now we have important business to attend to. As soon as Sophie appears with Mafalda on the steps, we have to bring the flowerpots back to their original position. That way the magic will be restored and the river specter will be caught again. Come on." They left the office and went through the hall. Before Hammond opened the front doors they both put on their sunglasses and plugged up their ears. From then on they would have to communicate with hand signals.

As Max stepped out of the castle, everything was clouded in brownish tones. It took a moment to get used to. Through the glasses, the sun looked like a rice cake. The park looked dark and spooky. But the steps and the flowerpots on the stairs were still recognizable.

Then Max saw a terrible sight.

There on the bottom step lay Sophie, the river specter kneeling over her.

"Sophie!" screamed Max. Even though he was wearing the earplugs he could still hear how Hammond yelled: "Mafalda!"

The river specter looked up. Triumphantly, she threw her arms into the air and showed her loot: the bejeweled, golden necklace.

Hammond gasped. "She has the gold. Now it's too late."

But Max didn't hear Hammond's words. He only had eyes for Sophie. Instinctively, he grabbed the worrystone from his pants' pocket. The stone was pulsating and warm. Max could feel the power that it emitted. And in that very moment he knew what he had to do.

He raced down the stairs, two steps at a time. The river specter moved her mouth and called to him, but Max didn't hear a thing, nor did he feel the irresistible urge to follow her—like he had the first time. But he did notice how Sophie sat up and slowly got to her feet.

Sophie's head was spinning. She couldn't think clearly, but at least the pain was gone from her neck. As she looked up she saw the gold sparkling above her. Sophie reacted immediately. She jumped from the ground, grabbing for the necklace.

It was obvious to Max why Sophie was such a good basketball player at school. Her teammates prized her quickness and determination as much as her opponents feared them.

The sneak attack was successful. Mafalda was so taken by surprise that Sophie was able to grab onto one end of the necklace. They both pulled and tugged at the gold until it broke in two and each held a piece in their hand.

Sophie lost her balance and fell against the stone banister. Mafalda stumbled as well. She tried to catch herself, but at the same time Max charged toward her and snatched the gold. Quick as lightning, he grabbed Sophie's arm and pulled her to her feet. They both ran down the steps, followed by the river specter, who was roaring with anger and stretching out her arms, first reaching toward Max and then toward Sophie.

Both Max and Sophie could feel the wetness that seeped out of Mafalda, smell the mold on her dress, and almost taste the salt of her hair. In the reflection of the sunglasses, Max could see that Hammond was crouching behind a flowerpot and signing to him: Go left!

Max understood and threw himself against the pot. One earplug popped out, so he heard Hammond bellowing: "Counterclockwise! A half turn!" Max shoved the pot. Suddenly Sophie was next to him and Hammond was pushing from the other side. Together they turned the flowerpot back to its original position.

Sophie looked up then and saw Mafalda. The river specter stiffened midstep, as if she had a sudden pain. Her face was turned up toward the sky, arms outstretched and fingers widespread. The green-and-gold cloak began to shimmer. Twigs sprouted left and right from her arms. Leaves grew from her fingers. Her blonde hair turned into a crown of branches. Mafalda's face began to change. Her expressions became more and more rigid as her skin turned to wood. One moment her face was still recognizable, the next it disappeared into gnarled bark. Suddenly a strong wind blew up out of nowhere. Mafalda's leaves were ripped away, twigs and branches twirled into the air, forming a green whirlwind that twisted faster and faster. Sophie became dizzy just looking at it. Then, just as suddenly, the wind stopped. The whirlwind sank to the ground. Only a small pile of leaves and bark was left behind. The river specter had completely disappeared.

Hammond took off his sunglasses and pulled out his earplugs.

"That's it," he said, and exhaled deeply. "Now Mafalda is back where she belongs."

Sophie shuddered. "Is she dead?"

"No, just banned from here by the ultimate power." Hammond eyed the flowerpots.

"Tomorrow we'll have to plant the pots again. It would probably be a good idea to cement them to the steps, so that no one inadvertently turns them."

"I am so very sorry," said Sophie guiltily. "I never would have guessed that it would have such consequences. I only wanted the ducks to look at each other." The hairs on the back of her neck stood on end as she thought about everything that had happened after her careless action.

"You owe us an explanation," Max said to Hammond, as he removed his sunglasses. "What is going on here? We want to know everything. Every detail."

Hammond nodded thoughtfully. "Yes, I suppose it's time. Come inside the castle. I will tell you everything."

# Ghost Park

They sat in the office. Both pieces of the broken necklace lay on the table. Amadeus Hammond reached for them and sighed. "I will have to send this to the Secret Council of 12. Along with a detailed letter about what happened today." He looked at both of them. "Give me your word of honor. You cannot tell a single soul what I am about to tell you."

"I can't promise anything," protested Max. "How can we be sure there isn't something here that the police should know about?"

"My young friend, in this case the police are completely helpless. You can be sure of that." Hammond cleared his throat. "Well then. I will rephrase my request. Please don't tell anyone about this."

Sophie and Max exchanged glances. A plea was something different. They could live with that, and so they both nodded their heads.

"Not a single word to your parents, siblings, friends, grandparents, to your minister, to your teachers, or anyone else," emphasized Hammond and leaned forward. "Even your pets shouldn't know anything about this."

Max stopped short. "Pets?"

"Haven't you ever heard of parrots that spill the

beans?" replied Hammond.

"Our little rabbit, Fluffy, can't even talk," said Max. "And we don't have any other animals."

"I don't have any pets at all," added Sophie.

"If the wrong person were to hear, the entire existence of this park would be called into question," said Hammond in a serious tone. "No one from the outside is supposed to know about it." He paused and took a deep breath. "This park is, well, a sort of zoo. Just not one for animals. We take care of ghosts and other beings related both to white and black magic."

Max and Sophie looked at one another. Ghosts! Beings! An entire zoo of them! It was as if someone had pulled the rug out from under their feet. In one moment everything that they had believed in was turned on its head. Sophie for her part wasn't sure whether she should feel sorry for herself or thank her lucky stars that she had become part of such an adventure.

And Max felt the same way. Until now, the laws of the universe had governed everything, and ghosts had belonged to the realm of fantasy. But now? Max was the first to speak. "Act-actually, I just wanted a job . . ."

"Me, too," added Sophie weakly.

"And you shall have it, too," promised Hammond.

"You shall work here and be paid for your work." He turned toward Sophie. "You, too, in case that wasn't entirely clear."

Sophie gave a half smile. This wasn't exactly what she had had in mind.

"One might say that you will have the opportunity

to expand your horizons," continued Hammond. "You won't be looking after just the gardens, but you'll also be taking care of the creatures in it."

"You mean creatures like Mafalda?" cried Sophie, horrified.

"Not all of them are like that," said Hammond, reassuringly. "Throughout the park there are also nice and helpful ghosts. For example, the Clingy-Ghosts. In principle, they are completely harmless. At most they cause a little mischief. Like my little Nepomuk, who you noticed during your first visit." Now Hammond looked at Max.

"That invisible thing that jumped up onto your shoulder?" asked Max.

"Exactly. Clingy-Ghosts need attention and stimulation, otherwise they get bored."

"And where are all of these ghosts?" Sophie wanted to know. "I didn't see anything special outside in the park—well, except for Malfada."

"Beneath the surface of the park, an entirely different world exists. A second level you might say," Hammond explained.

"Like with computer games," said Max.

"A ghost level," mumbled Sophie. "Well, thanks a lot."

"I don't really know my way around computers. Although," he paused and knocked on the screen to his right, "I am finding that I had better get used to them." He switched on the computer. It started up slowly, and gradually rows and rows of numbers and letters appeared on the screen.

"Just as lame as the one in my house," mumbled Max.

"Yes, but it still does its job." Hammond drummed his fingers on the desktop. "There have always been magic creatures. For centuries. Actually, since the beginning of time. The sagas and legends tell of them. For example Lilith, Adam's first wife. Or Lamien. Those are the precursors to vampires. Dragons. Poltergeists. Nymphs. There are too many kinds to count. Many evolved on their own. But others were created artificially in a laboratory or were called to life through magic. Most of the beings mean no harm to humans, but there are those who do want to hurt us. There is one constant however: the magical creatures are not tolerated in the human realm. They are stalked, threatened, driven out. Many have been completely eradicated. Therefore, a long time ago, it was decided to create special protective zones for these creatures."

"Like a kind of wildlife preserve," said Sophie

"Or a national park," added Max.

"Yes," confirmed Hammond. "Except that here humans are normally forbidden from entering. We don't want any visitors or curious guests. Only caretakers and guardians are permitted." He paused for a moment. "The parks are controlled by the Secret Council of 12."

"And who are they?" asked Sophie.

"I don't know if I should burden you with that yet," Hammond said, more to himself, but then he shrugged. "One day you will know about it anyway. The Secret

Council of 12 is a group of the most powerful magicians of white and black magic. They are elected every 13 years."

"Magicians," repeated Max. Everything sounded so unbelievable! First, they had to come to terms with ghosts and now they had to accept that apparently there were also a bunch of magicians who had amazing powers.

"These 12 magicians reached an agreement with one another. They have promised never to use the creatures in the park for their own means," said Hammond. "The parks were created to preserve the diversity of the creatures and to assure their well-being. Aha, finally!" he exclaimed leaning toward the screen.

The computer was ready. "Come over here, I want to show you something."

As Sophie and Max pulled their chairs over to the desk, Hammond typed on the keyboard and reached for the mouse. Very slowly, a picture of the castle appeared on the screen. Finally, the picture was complete. Hammond clicked again. Then a colored map of the park's layout slowly built itself upon the screen. Green areas and flower beds were layered one upon another. The castle was centered in the middle of the picture. From there, several paths branched. Some created a geometric pattern; others produced a totally twisted shape. Sophie recognized the dolphin pond and the part of the park in which she had started her adventure with Mafalda.

"That's how the grounds would look to an ordinary

visitor," said Hammond, and scrolled up. "It was laid out by a former owner of the castle in the 18th century."

According to the map, the park was huge!

"Rose garden," Max read out loud, as the map rolled upwards on the screen. "Orangerie, Labyrinth, South Park."

Hammond clicked on a circle. A window appeared on the screen, and he typed in a 13-digit password. Then the picture began to refresh itself. The same outlines could be seen, but the captions were completely different.

Again Max read from the screen: "Alley of Dreams, Gated Garden, Witches' Cauldron, Monster Hill, Department of Small Ghosts, Bottle Ghost Collection."

"This is the level that lies beneath the surface of the actual park," explained Hammond. "It exists at the same time as the normal grounds. Level one and level two are connected to each other by magical doors. One level can't exist without the other. Together they form an inseparable unity."

"Aha," said Max. Certain things were now starting to make sense, like the bewitched plot of earth he had dug up and the gate in the hedge, a gate that could appear and disappear again. Now Hammond explained how the owner of the castle was supposed to carry full responsibility for the park.

"That's how it has always been in the past. Unfortunately, we have a bit of a problem right now. We are unable to find the genuine owner. The previous owner

died a while back, and he had a son who was supposedly in America. But we can't find any trace of him. So in the meantime, I was appointed supervisor. I promised the old owner of the castle, upon his deathbed, that I would take care of everything until the rightful heir appeared." Hammond stopped speaking and all of a sudden looked exhausted.

"Can't you just search for him on the Internet?" suggested Max.

"Believe me, we have tried every possibility," answered Hammond with a sigh. "One day we will find him, of that I am certain. The question is when. And because the work here lately has become too much for me, the Secret Council of 12 allowed me to search for an assistant." He smiled and gazed at both of the children. "And now I have two. Even better."

Sophie fidgeted in her chair. She wasn't sure she wanted the job. "And what are we supposed to do? This all sounds pretty dangerous . . ."

"It's certainly not child's play," said Hammond. "But I am convinced that you are the right ones for the job, even though you are a little young. I gave Max a little entrance exam. And you . . ." He looked at Sophie. "Well, anyone who can beat Mafalda can also care for Ghost Park! But certainly I understand that you both may have some reservations." He clicked off the computer and abruptly stood up. "Perhaps it would be best if I took you on a small tour."

# The Alley of Dreams

"Actually, I've already had enough excitement for one day," whispered Max to Sophie, as they followed Hammond through the corridor.

Sophie nodded. "Not just for today, but for the next few weeks as well," she whispered. "What happens if we just leave?"

"I have no idea," Max answered quietly. "But if Hammond sends the Secret Council of 12 after us, we certainly won't have anything to laugh about."

Deep down, however, Max and Sophie knew they were officially part of the park now and couldn't just act as if the whole thing wasn't their concern. Their lives had simply changed. They couldn't deny the existence of ghosts anymore. Even if they tried to forget everything, it would be impossible. Sophie was sure that even as a 70-year-old woman she would remember Mafalda.

"White and black magic," whispered Sophie. "I never really thought there were such things."

"Me, neither."

They left the castle and followed Hammond down the steps. Sophie looked at the empty flowerpots with both awe and apprehension. She certainly wouldn't touch them again!

Now the wind had blown most of the leaves from the stairs. The sun hung low in the sky. Hammond kept on walking. They turned south and soon came to an alley of mighty poplars, still bare, that seemed to extend into infinity.

"We're here," announced Hammond. "This is one of the magical doors to Ghost Park. In order to enter into the Alley of Dreams, one has to go backward but think forward."

Max and Sophie stared at Hammond.

"Go backward and think forward?" repeated Max. "How's that supposed to work?"

"Go backward is clear," said Hammond and took a few steps backward. "And thinking forward means that you have to think about something that will happen in the future: tomorrow, next week, next year . . ."

"Like, maybe Christmas?" asked Sophie.

"Yes, Christmas would work," said Hammond. "The main thing is that you concentrate. You'll have to practice a bit at the beginning."

Sophie didn't think that sounded too difficult.

"Good luck," Hammond said. "See you in the Alley of Dreams."

With every step backward, his outline grew fainter. Slowly, he seemed to fade and then suddenly disappeared altogether.

"Unbelievable," whispered Max in awe.

Sophie nodded. "Should we go, too?" she asked. "Or should we just grab our bikes and get out of here?

This would be the perfect opportunity."

Max thought about it for a moment. On one hand, he was scared of the unknown, but on the other hand, he found it fascinating. Ghost Park piqued his curiosity. "Honestly, I'm ready to risk it," he said at last.

"Me, too," confessed Sophie.

They grinned at each other. This was why they were friends. They often shared the same opinion.

"Okay then, how did it go?" asked Max. "Forward thinking and backward going."

He and Sophie started to step backward. Sophie tried to imagine the upcoming Christmas party. But then she caught herself. She had let her thoughts wander to last Christmas. She remembered the in-line skates she had gotten.

"Wrong!" she said and shook her head. Hammond was right. It wasn't all that simple! She tried to really concentrate this time. What events lay in the near future?

Then she remembered the math test.

She imagined how Mr. Kern would come through the door and hand out the tests. There would surely be four parts, further divided into two sections. There might also be a scrawled drawing that no one could figure out. Sophie saw how she would stare at the paper and how she would begin to feel tortured. Her brain would be replaced with a gaping hole. Cluelessly, she would scrawl a few numbers on the paper . . .

As she thought about it, she noticed that all around her things were growing dimmer. With every step backward, the sky darkened. It was a totally unnatural darkness, like a storm that suddenly appears . . . was she already crossing over into Ghost Park?

"Concentrate!" Sophie told herself. She didn't want to get distracted. She forced herself to think about the math test again.

The minutes on the school clock were ticking away, but still she didn't have the answers. Soon, Mr. Kern would be standing next to her desk, and he would take away her paper with an arrogant smile.

"Well, Sophie, another disaster? I've never had such a lost case in my class before. I'm going to speak to your other teachers, so that they can remove you from school . . ."

What was that? The bare trees had disappeared. Sophie was actually sitting in her classroom and Mr.

Kern stood before her in living color—with his plaid shirt and the poorly fitting gray pants, the belt hidden under his large belly.

"You will spend the entire night in detention . . ."

Sophie looked out of the window. Outside it was pitch-black. She was the only one left in the classroom. It smelled like chalk and floor polish. The other chairs had been put on top of the desks. Mr. Kern slipped behind the podium, pulled out a newspaper, and began to read. Sophie's heart pounded in her ears. "But, but my parents will be worried if I don't come home . . ."

Mr. Kern's face appeared above the edge of the paper. What a repelling grin! "You can leave the room, but only after you have solved each problem—without any mistakes!"

"I-I-I can't do it," stammered Sophie. Mr. Kern was asking the impossible.

"Get to work!" thundered the math teacher.

"Get to work, get to work," echoed in Sophie's ears, louder and louder, until her head roared and everything around her turned black. Sophie burst into tears. She had tried her hardest . . .

"Sophie! Hey, Sophie!"

Someone was shaking her arm. She opened her eyes. It was still as night all around her.

"It's me, Max!"

A flashlight suddenly brightened the darkness. Sophie saw Max sitting next to her, holding onto her arm. Behind them stood Hammond, shining the light around them.

"We're here," said Max.

"Oh, Max." Sophie noticed how shaky her voice sounded. "I just saw Mr. Kern, he was going to force me to stay in the classroom all night . . ."

"A dream," said Hammond.

"It wasn't much better for me," Max told her. "I imagined that someone had kidnapped my little sister and that the police were at our house. It was really terrible!"

"Everyone who steps into the Alley of Dreams experiences whatever they are most afraid of," said Hammond. "But they are just dreams and therefore there is no real danger. It is actually a harmless part of Ghost Park. Among the trees here live the night owls. They are not dangerous. Their strength comes from the pure power of thought. They won't bite, but they can sense and intensify your inner fears."

"Oh, great," said Sophie. Hammond could've warned her about the night owls before. "What did you dream about?" she asked the old man, but Hammond only mumbled something about the Secret Council of 12, and then said, "Let's go on."

"Any more surprises waiting?" asked Max suspiciously.

"Not in the Alley of Dreams," replied Hammond.

"You should call it the Alley of Nightmares," mumbled Sophie. "Heart attacks and strokes are the door prizes."

"I thought you were brave and fearless," Hammond answered lightly. "By the way—the more often you go

through the Alley of Dreams, the more certain you become that it's all a dream."

Sophie and Max exchanged glances. Neither of them had the slightest desire to go through the Alley of Dreams again.

"Are there other doors?" Sophie asked.

"Of course," answered Hammond. "But that was the easiest and least dangerous entrance."

Together, Sophie and Max followed Hammond, who had resumed the tour and was lighting the way with the flashlight.

It was exactly the opposite of before. With every step forward, it got lighter and the darkness faded away. Soon they didn't need the flashlight at all. Sophie and Max saw huge trees surrounding them—trees that were taller and bigger than the poplars in the castle's garden. The branches were already covered in leaves as if the seasons had no place here.

Max glanced about for the night owls. He had no idea what they might look like, and he was curious. High in the branches, he managed to glimpse an owl-like shape with thick white plumage like a snow owl. But it appeared to have only one large eye above a yellow beak. Suddenly, the night owl blinked, realizing it had been discovered, and instantly hid itself among the leaves again.

"Night owls are quite shy," Hammond said then. "They are afraid of everything. The nightmares they give you are a kind of self-defense, not really anything evil. It's just automatic for them." Now Max felt sorry for the night owls. It must be terrible to be afraid of everything all of the time.

"We're approaching the Department of Small Ghosts," said Hammond as they reached the end of the alley. Before them was a circular flower bed in front of several pavilions. Some of the pavilions had wrought iron bars and looked like cages. Others had proper walls with doors and windows.

In the first cage squatted a row of strange monkey-like creatures in a multitude of colors from pink to orange to lavender. Most of the beings had wings. As they neared the cage, they started to jump and fly against the bars, shrieking and wailing loudly.

"Pests," explained Hammond. "There are countless varieties. Inside here we have Poison-Spitters, Short-Tempered Ghosts, Snorting-with-Rage Ghosts, and Pain-in-the-Necks." Sophie and Max watched the fascinating little creatures. They all had sharp teeth and flat batlike noses.

"Pests are found around the entire world," continued Hammond. "They live unseen among humans. Almost every household will get one sometime. They are extremely difficult to get rid of."

A Short-Tempered Ghost stuck out his pointed tongue at Hammond. At the same time a little Snorting-with-Rage Ghost spit purple mucus out of the cage. Max took a step back. "Nice," he said.

"They get quite upset when someone sees them," Hammond explained. "They like it much better when they are invisible."

Hammond moved on to the next cage, in which colorful birds were flying. At first, Sophie thought they were woodpeckers, because they were hammering and poking at branches placed inside the cage. But when she got closer she saw that the birds had strange growths under their wings, rather than feet.

90

"These are the Bellyachers." Hammond knocked against the bars, and instantly the birds reacted with intolerable squawking. "They are always hanging around and complaining about the same thing. Highly annoying. And they reproduce quite easily."

The next pavilion was locked. Hammond took out a key, opened the door, and they stepped into a six-cornered room with two glass display cases. One was filled with all kinds of bottles, from beer bottles to fancy perfume bottles. The other held several varieties of lamps: tiny oil lamps, flashlights, table lamps, and kerosene lanterns.

"Our reserve of bottle and lamp ghosts." Hammond shone the flashlight over the cases. "In every bottle and lamp is a ghost just waiting to be freed and to serve. These ghosts give their new master anything his heart desires."

"What a waste that they're just sitting around here," whispered Max in Sophie's ear. "I could really use a

bottle ghost, couldn't you?"

Sophie nodded. "He could do my homework, clean my room, go in my place to school—it would really be quite practical."

"The ghosts have to be let out every once in a while or else they grow impatient," Hammond said wiping the dust from the display case. "But, unfortunately, it's quite dangerous. Sometimes, a bottle ghost has had time to stew over things while in the bottle, and he wants to break the neck of the very person who frees him."

Sophie shivered. She wasn't about to uncork a bottle anytime soon!

"It's pretty much the same thing with the lamp ghosts," said Hammond, going over to the other case. "But lamp ghosts grow impatient even more quickly. Those that are obviously dangerous are brought down to Department Four. It's the place where special security measures must be taken. You'll see it another time. I think you've seen enough for your first day."

Max was relieved. His head was buzzing from the strange sights.

"I'll show you just one more thing," said Hammond with a sudden soft expression in his face. "Something beautiful. Quite rare actually."

They left the pavilion and entered the building across the way after Hammond had unlocked it. The room was entirely empty except for a large aquarium sitting atop a glass table. Hammond brought a finger to his lips and motioned to the children that they should walk quietly toward the aquarium.

At first, Max and Sophie didn't see anything but aquatic plants. Then a sea horse swam near the glass, and the surface of the water rippled. Suddenly, a little nymph appeared above the water and swam toward the glass. She grabbed on to the edge, pulled herself up, and sat on the top of the aquarium. She had long blond hair and a silvery-green fishtail that glittered in the light. Sophie had never seen anything so beautiful. She watched mesmerized, as the nymph pulled a tiny comb from between her scales and began to comb her hair, humming quietly. After a moment, a tiny merman appeared swimming between the aquatic plants and up to the surface. He had a green beard and his chest was covered with thick green hair. In his hand, he held a triton, but it wasn't any bigger than a kitchen fork. He glided over to the mermaid and she bent down and gave him a kiss.

Sophie was so delighted that she let out a little cry. Instantly, the pair dove back into the water and disappeared. "I'm sorry," said Sophie with a sigh. "But they were just so cute!"

"Those are Nelly and Nock, the last of their kind," Hammond explained. "There are none like them in the entire world. They were artificially created in the Middle Ages in a laboratory.

We have been hoping for years that they might have children of their own, but so far it hasn't happened."

Sophie wished she could take the mini-mermaid and the mini-merman home with her. She had never seen anything so enchanting. "They are so beautiful," she murmured, as they stood in front of the pavilion again, her thoughts still on the dainty creatures.

"I knew I had to show you Nelly and Nock so you would realize that there are creatures that can create feelings very different from fear," said Hammond. "Maybe now you'll look forward to your work." Sophie and Max exchanged a glance.

"Maybe," said Max, and Sophie nodded.

"That's enough for today," said Hammond again. "I suggest we take the Cerberus Catapult. That's the quickest way to get back to the castle."

"Cerberus Catapult?" asked Max and Sophie in unison.

"You'll see it in a bit. Come along."

# In the Cerberus Catapult

They left the circle of pavilions. Max glanced over his shoulder. He would have liked to stay and see the other pavilions, but he thought Sophie looked exhausted. He couldn't blame her. She had certainly spent a lot of energy trying to capture Mafalda. And she had saved his life.

"Would you like to get an ice cream after this? My treat," he whispered to her.

"How can you think about ice cream at a time like this?" Sophie cried.

"I just meant . . ."

"I couldn't eat ice cream right now if you paid me!" announced Sophie. "My stomach is in knots and the goose bumps on my arms are permanent. And now we have to go through a Cerberus Catapult. That sounds pretty scary, don't you think?"

Max shrugged his shoulders. "I don't know."

Sophie sighed. "Do you even know who Cerberus was? He was in this movie I saw a while ago with my dad. Cerberus was a three-headed monstrous dog in Greek mythology. He guarded the underworld. A huge, mean beast. No one could get in or out without going by him first. I'm not sure I want to see such a terrible creature!"

"Oh, come on," Max said cheerfully. "It can't be that bad."

"Do you know what I want? My bed, my pajamas, a glass of warm milk with a little honey, and a big bar of chocolate. Then I will be happy. I want to sleep for at least 12 hours without dreaming of a single ghost!"

"Where are you kids?" called Hammond.

Max realized the old man was far ahead of them now.

"We're coming," he called and grabbed Sophie's arm. "Look, you've done great so far. And anyway, it's almost over."

"That's what you think," said Sophie, but she let Max pull her along.

Hammond had stopped in front of a rocky hill. Max wanted to ask where the Cerberus Catapult was, but just then an opening appeared in the middle of the rocks.

"A mouth," said Sophie flatly. "That is nothing but a huge and dreadful mouth. I knew it." Now Max and Sophie could see that the hill was actually a huge dog's head. Tufts of grass grew out from the nostrils. The eyes were black shiny plates, practically hidden behind the bushy eyebrows that looked like burnt undergrowth.

"This is the shortest way back," announced Hammond. "We'll land directly in the castle." He gestured to them to step inside of the mouth.

Max and Sophie hesitated, examining the huge cavity. Gigantic teeth sprouted from the jaw, just like stalactites and stalagmites in a cave. In the middle lay

a panting tongue. Sophie took a step back.

"Cerberus doesn't do anything," Hammond assured her. "He just stops the ghosts from bolting. Normally, level-changers like ourselves pass through undisturbed."

"I'm not going in there," insisted Sophie. "I don't have a death wish. I guarantee you, he'll eat us up. I don't want to be dog food."

"I give you my word of honor that Cerberus is completely harmless," said Hammond. "I hired you both because I need you. Would it make sense for me to put you in unnecessary danger?"

Sophie and Max glanced at one another.

"That's true," said Max. "It's logical. I trust him."

"Can't we go back through the Alley of Dreams?" asked Sophie. Suddenly the thought of having to face her math teacher again wasn't nearly as bad as the thought of sticking one of her legs into the mouth of the frightening dog.

"Unfortunately, the Alley of Dreams is a one-way street," answered Hammond. "You can enter Ghost Park through its magical door, but you can't get out the same way."

Sophie bit her lip. "Are you sure it's not dangerous?" she asked one last time.

Hammond smiled. "Just be careful not to slip on his tongue or slide into his throat. If that happens you'll be swallowed and land in a deeply magical realm. And then it's a little more complicated to get you back. We would need at least three members from the Secret Council of 12 to do that. But it's not impossible."

Sophie swallowed and Max turned pale.

"Deeply magical realm?" Max repeated.

"Come on," Sophie said after taking a deep breath. "We won't slip. Let's go, or I'll never get to my bed and glass of milk."

Hammond went first and Max and Sophie followed close behind. It was a strange feeling to step into the dark mouth. The huge tongue was soft and it moved underneath their feet. It felt as if they were standing aboard a ship. A putrid gust of wind greeted them— the breath of the beast.

"Hold onto the teeth," advised Hammond as he switched his flashlight back on. All around them Max and Sophie saw reddish-purple marble walls. The ground beneath them continued to move. Once Sophie slipped and grabbed hold of the nearest tooth. Imme-

diately, she pulled back, wiping her hands on her pants and shivering in disgust.

"Do you see that thing up there?" Hammond pointed in the air. Far above hung a reddish cone. "That's his uvula. To get back to the castle, we must tickle it."

Before Max and Sophie could ask any further questions, Hammond had climbed on top of the teeth and was touching the pink cone. Immediately everything around them started to move. Max and Sophie held on to one another. From the depths of the monster came a dull growl, then it coughed. Sophie and Max were catapulted through utter blackness. They could not see or hear a thing.

"Help!" squeaked Sophie, blindly feeling around her. "MAX! Where are you?" Then she landed with a bump on the floor. She blinked. The chandelier hung above her. She was in the castle, in the middle of the pentagram. Max and Hammond had landed behind her, safe and sound. Hammond stood and brushed the dust from his pants. "Didn't I tell you? The Cerberus Catapult is the quickest way back. It wasn't so bad, was it?"

# Home Again

"Well, I don't know," Sophie said a little later to Max, as they pushed their bikes out of the park gate. "I can't believe everything that happened really happened. Maybe it was all just a dream—or a nightmare! Pinch me."

Max did as he had been told. Sophie grimaced. "But if you dream you are being pinched, it also hurts in the dream. I guess that doesn't prove anything."

Max turned around again. "Look." He pointed to the hedge. The gate, through which they had just come, had suddenly disappeared. Not a trace of it was visible.

"Well, I guess that means we didn't make up the whole thing," sighed Sophie.

"I'm afraid not," answered Max. "What do you think? Should we ever come back?"

"We have a couple of days to think about it," said Sophie. "Hammond isn't expecting us until Monday."

They got on their bikes and pedaled home. Along the way, the events of the day played themselves out like a film in front of Sophie's eyes: the evergreen ducks, Mafalda, Max lying still on the ground, the golden necklace used to lure the river specter, the creatures inside the pavilions . . .

Sophie braked so hard that Max almost crashed into her rear tire. "I bet we just saw a little piece. Ghost Park must be huge!" she exclaimed.

"I was just thinking that, too," said Max. "What about Department Four. I wonder what goes on in there."

"Nelly and Nock were so adorable," said Sophie dreamily. "I definitely have to see them again."

"And the Cerberus Catapult wasn't actually that bad," said Max. "It was really convenient to land in the middle of the castle."

They looked at one another.

"Monday afternoon at three?" asked Max.

Sophie grinned. "I guess so."

They started pedaling again. At the corner of Max's street, they went their separate ways, waving good-bye to one another.

"I'll call you tomorrow morning," yelled Max.

"But not before eleven," Sophie called back. "I want to sleep in!"

As soon as Max had parked his bike and stepped inside the front door, his mother appeared. "You're late," she said. Then she noticed Max's clothing. "What happened?"

Max looked down at his clothes, still caked with mud in places. "I got a little dirty. I'm sorry."

"Take off your shoes before you get the floor dirty," said his mother. "And wash your hands. You may as well just throw your clothes straight into the hamper."

Max went into the bathroom and glanced at himself

in the mirror. Except for looking a little tired, he looked as he always had. No one would ever know that in one afternoon his entire life had changed.

Julia burst through the door. "Your dinner is getting cold," she announced.

"Can't you knock?" asked Max.

"Hey, where'd you get that pretty stone?" she cried, looking at the worrystone that Max had placed next to the sink.

"I found it," Max answered.

"Can I have it?" Julia reached her hand out longingly.

"You can look at it," said Max, reluctantly handing her the stone.

Julia examined it with interest, tracing the symbols with her index finger. "Do you want to trade?" she begged. "I'll give you my pink shell for it."

Max really liked his little sister, but he couldn't give up the worrystone. He would certainly need it again in Ghost Park. "I don't think so."

"What if I give you my silver medal?" Julia had won the medal at a raffle, and it was her most prized possession.

"I can't trade anything for it," explained Max. "That's not a normal stone. I mean, it found me—that's why I have to keep it."

"It found you?" repeated Julia, unbelieving.

"Well, it's sort of a magic stone, get it?"

Julia's eyes twinkled. "A magic stone?"

"Max, Julia, where are you?" called their mother from the kitchen. "Are you coming or not?"

Max quickly ran to his room to put on clean clothes. He tucked the stone in his pocket again. The spinach on his plate was ice-cold, but Max ate it up without a fight. His dad announced that he was going to build a new hutch for their rabbit.

"Hey, I got a job," said Max, when they were finished with dinner and clearing the plates.

"A job?" his mother asked. "What is it?"

"I'm helping an old man with his garden," answered Max carefully. It wasn't exactly a lie. At least it was partly true.

"Sophie is helping, too."

"Well, you should've asked for permission first," scolded his mother. "How often will you be going there? Will you still have enough time for your schoolwork? Who is this man and how did you find the job?"

Luckily, Max's father was on his side. "I think that this is fantastic. You'll get a lot of fresh air. And it's healthier than sitting behind a computer."

If they only knew, thought Max.

"Sophie's parents don't have a problem with it?" asked his mother.

"I don't think so."

"Well, we'll see what happens," said Mrs. Hope. "If your schoolwork suffers, then you'll have to stop."

"I'll stay on top of everything," replied Max.

"Let's hope you do!" his mother said. Then she turned to Julia. "Now, go straight to the bathroom and then to bed. You don't get to stay up so late every night."

Julia slid from her chair. "Can Max read me a story?"

"Sure," answered Max.

"But don't tell her any scary stories," warned his mother. "I know you like to do that."

"Don't worry," Max said, giving Julia a wink.

Julia grinned. "I'm never scared," she whispered.

"Well then, hurry up." Max gave his sister a gentle shove. "I'll be there in five minutes."

Julia disappeared into the bathroom. A fleck of tooth-paste was stuck in the corner of her mouth when Max sat down on her bed a little later. Max wiped it away.

"Will you show me the magic stone again?" begged Julia.

Max sighed and pulled the worrystone from his pocket. "Here, but be very careful with it." He took Julia's favorite book from the nightstand. "And which story would the royal princess like tonight?"

Julia sighed happily as she held the stone in her hand.

"Make something up. But it has to be really scary!"

# Book II

# The Imposter

# So Long, Job?

"Can't she ever put the cap back on?" mumbled Max under his breath. It was annoying how his little sister, Julia, never remembered to close the toothpaste correctly.

"Hurry up, Max," called Mrs. Hope from the hallway. "You'll be late for school!" Max squeezed some dried-out toothpaste onto his toothbrush and brushed his teeth with his right hand while combing his hair with his left. Thirty seconds later, with freshly combed hair and minty-fresh breath, he left the bathroom and ran directly into the jacket his mom held out to him like a bullfighter holding a red cape in front of a bull.

"C'mon, hop to it!" Mrs. Hope commanded.

Max's arms were hardly in the sleeves before he had his backpack on and was pushed in the direction of the front door. Meanwhile, Julia was whining that she couldn't find her right boot.

"Here it is, in the umbrella stand!" said Max, fishing out the missing boot.

Mom groaned and jiggled the car keys impatiently. She worked as a secretary at the high school and dropped Julia off at preschool on her way to work. Mr. Hope stayed at home, took care of Fluffy, their rabbit, and searched the newspaper for a new job. There weren't a lot of jobs open for cabinetmakers.

This morning, Mr. Hope had laid out a few boards and some of his tools in the living room. He wanted to build Fluffy a bigger cage. Mom didn't seem especially pleased with this. Max knew that she would rather see Dad acting a little more eager to find a job. But Max thought it was totally normal that his father was at home. He cooked very well. He did the vacuuming and the laundry. His favorite thing, though, was to build beautiful stuff out of wood. Unfortunately, no one was paying him money to do that right now so money was awfully tight for the Hope family.

Max was happy that he would be earning money at his new job—even if the job was a little strange. He couldn't wait to go back to the castle that afternoon. He hoped Hammond would show them more ghosts. He wondered if Sophie felt the same way.

"Are you still dreaming, Max?" Mrs. Hope was growing impatient. "I asked you if you packed your lunch. Where is your mind today?"

"On ghosts," answered Max truthfully.

"Oh, great!" yelled Julia, hopping up and down around Max. "Can you tell me a new story tonight? One that's really super gruesome?"

"You and your ghosts," sighed his mom. "Honestly, Max, you are getting too old for fairy tales!"

Max was 12. He didn't think age had anything to do with whether someone believed in ghosts or not. What would his mother do if suddenly a nice spirit materialized before her very eyes? Or what if a ghost appeared in school when Mr. Kern was giving his students a test? Mr. Kern was Max and Sophie's math teacher. Sophie, Max's best friend, had started off the school year on the wrong foot with him.

"C'mon, c'mon, c'mon," urged Max's mom as she shoved Max through the door. "School starts in a few minutes. Hurry up, will you? Or do you have the day off?"

"It's a ghost day," squeaked Julia. "Sometimes there's no school because it's too hot. So maybe if there are ghosts, it's a ghost day!"

"Julia, it's the beginning of March," said Mrs. Hope sternly. "You won't have a day off because of the heat for a long time. And you'll certainly never have one off because of ghosts." She turned to Max. "Thanks to your stories, Max, your sister believes in ghosts!

"I'd better go! Don't want to be late!" called Max as he rushed down the steps. On his way to school he wondered if Julia suspected anything. He had to be careful what he said, even if he told her stories just for fun. Julia must not get suspicious. No one from his family must have the slightest suspicion!

"Excited?" asked Max, as he and Sophie got off their bicycles later that afternoon. The large wrought iron gate to 29 Juniper Way towered before them. Today they had had no trouble finding the gate. Sometimes the gate simply disappeared. At those times you could ride back and forth as long as you wanted beside the high hedge and never find the entrance to the park.

"A little," answered Sophie. "Aren't you?"

"Oh, sure." Max opened the gate, which groaned quietly on its hinges. They pushed their bikes on the gravel path. As they rounded the bend in the path, the castle appeared before them. Shimmering in the sun, it looked beautiful and serene. The grass around the castle already showed a hint of spring. White, yellow, and violet crocuses peeked up through the bright green grass.

No one would guess that a secret ghost world hid itself within the park.

"What do you think we'll have to do today?" asked

Sophie. "Clean up ghost poop?"

Max looked at her and made a face. "Maybe." He hadn't thought about that. "Maybe we'll have to feed the pests. Or let out the bottle ghosts so they can move around a little. I'm sure Hammond will tell us where to begin."

They locked their bikes and climbed up the wide steps to the castle's entrance. Max opened the double doors with the lion head knockers. They entered the large entrance hall and crossed over the black marble floor with the pentagram.

When they came to Hammond's office, Max knocked on the door. There was no answer from inside, so he turned the door handle. No one was in the office.

"Hammond isn't here," said Max in surprise. "But he knew that we were coming at three. Did he forget about us?"

Sophie shrugged her shoulders. "Maybe he's teaching the Short-Tempered Ghosts yodeling and is getting totally frustrated that they can't get it." She went around the desk that was normally covered in papers. Curious, she picked up a letter that was lying next to the computer and hastily scanned its lines.

"He must have received this today. It has yesterday's date on the top."

Max fidgeted. "Leave that alone, Sophie. It belongs to Hammond."

But Sophie didn't seem to hear. "Listen to this, Max."

*To the honorable Mr. Hammond,*

*Recently, word of my father's death reached me. I am deeply distressed and full of grief. I will come immediately to assume control of the inheritance. I am grateful that you have taken the utmost care of the castle and especially the park. In the future I will bear the responsibility. I will arrive on Tuesday, and we can make all necessary arrangements.*

*Sincerely yours,*
*Jonathan von Fleuch*

Sophie let the letter fall and stared at Max.

"Well, yeah," Max stuttered, "I guess that's normal. I mean the park does—in the end—belong to him. Hammond is just—"

Sophie didn't let him finish. "What do you think? Are we out of a job?" That had been Max's first thought, too.

"Maybe," said Max with a gloomy expression. "The castle's new owner is definitely younger than Hammond and might not need our help."

"It's not fair!" blurted Sophie. "We just started." Furious, she put the letter back on the desk.

"Come on, let's go look for Hammond," Max suggested. "He's probably just working outside somewhere." They left the castle, but they couldn't find the old man outside, either.

"Maybe he's busy feeding the Poison-Spitters and the Snorting-with-Rage Ghosts," suggested Sophie.

"Possibly," replied Max. "So now what?"

Sophie gave him a sly look. "Well, we know how to get into Ghost Park."

"You mean . . ." Max cleared his throat. "You mean, we should . . . on our own . . . ?"

"Sure, why not. Or would you rather go home?"

Max thought about it and shook his head.

"Okay," said Sophie. "Then let's go to the alley."

# A Newcomer in Ghost Park

The endless alley of long poplars was one of the magic gateways. From there one could enter Ghost Park through the Alley of Dreams.

Max reached for Sophie's hand. Not because he was scared, but because it made him feel more secure.

"Do you remember how to do it?" asked Sophie.

Max nodded. "Go backward and think forward."

Hand in hand, they stepped backward. Sophie could feel her knees growing weak. She knew that very soon they would be having a nightmare. She told herself not to forget that it was just a dream. Maybe it wouldn't be so bad after all.

"I'm thinking about tonight," mumbled Max. "I'm going to tell Julia a story."

"Shhhhhh," whispered Sophie. If Max was talking, she couldn't concentrate. She wondered which future event she should imagine. She thought of Hammond. She thought about how the old man would soon be greeting her and Max. She could see his wrinkled face again, his snow-white hair . . .

"It's good that you both are here," she heard his raspy old man's voice. "It's about time. The ghosts in Department Four are particularly uneasy . . ."

"What's that!?" Sophie suddenly heard another voice. Two large hands grabbed Hammond, lifted him high, and simply pushed him to the side. "We don't need any ghost caretakers!" A finger poked into Sophie's breastbone and a bearded face appeared before her. "I inherited this castle. Ghost Park belongs to me, and I decide what will happen with it. And right now I want you both to go home, and I mean NOW!"

"No, please," begged Sophie. "Please!"

The man shook his head. "It's out of the question! YOU HAVE NO BUSINESS IN GHOST PARK!"

A dream—the words shot through Sophie's head. It's just a dream. "You scram!" she yelled loudly. "Get out of here, you big meanie! You're just a dream!"

"Me? A DREAM? I'll prove to you I'm not, little girl!"

The man grabbed Sophie with both hands and threw her into the air. She somersaulted, but managed to land on her feet. "Ooohhh . . ." Her knees were wobbly as pudding, and her heart was beating like a drum.

Max was standing beside her, peering at her with a worried expression on his face.

"Is everything alright, Sophie?" he asked.

Sophie blew a few strands of hair out of her face and nodded. "I'm okay. What about you?"

"I was telling Julia a bedtime story, and suddenly she changed into a horrible river specter. I wanted to run away, but then I realized that it was just a dream," explained Max. "But it was pretty bad all the same."

"It was bad for me, too," agreed Sophie. "But at least it was better than last time."

They walked through the forest, still holding hands. Something rustled in the trees above their heads, and Sophie knew the night owls were watching them. When the path came to an end, Max and Sophie were at the pavilion filled with cages. The little ghosts were making quite a racket, screeching and flapping against the bars, just as they had before.

"Hammond's up ahead," called Sophie excitedly and pulled Max along. Hammond was pacing back and forth on the gravel path. He was holding a furry brown creature in his arms, petting it and speaking softly to it all the while. He was so preoccupied that he only noticed Max and Sophie when they were standing directly in front of him.

"Hello, Mr. Hammond!" they said.

The old man looked up, surprised. "You found the way all by yourselves?" There was no time to answer because the furry brown creature began to wail, franti-

cally clutching at Hammond's shoulder.

"Boo-hoo-hoo," it howled, tears spurting out in all
different directions. "Boo-hoo-hoo . . ." Sophie's heart
ached with sympathy.

"Do either of you have a tissue?" asked Hammond.

Max felt around in his pocket and handed him one.
Hammond took it and dried the face of the little creature. Its sobs became a little quieter as the critter
grabbed the tissue and slowly tore it into little bits.

"It's a Stone-Softener," Hammond told the children.
"It just arrived. A very rare ghost. There are, at most,
only three left on earth. The special thing about this
ghost is . . ."

"Boo-hoo-hoo," bawled the Stone-Softener again, and
the tears flowed once more. "No one loves Boo-hoo . . .
hoo-hoo . . . hoo-hoo . . ."

Sophie stretched out her arms to the little beast.
Hammond gave her the ghost, obviously happy to be

rid of it for a while.

"That it cries?" Max finished Hammond's sentence.

Hammond nodded. "Not only that. His tears dissolve every kind of stone. They simply liquefy them. They can even melt through the thickest concrete."

The Stone-Softener nestled against Sophie. She felt his warm little head against her throat. Then he peered curiously into her face. She saw two big blue eyes, already half-filled with tears, a nose that was pressed flat like a koala bear's, and a mouth like a chimpanzee's. There was something human about it, and in that very moment it appeared to feel all of the suffering in the world. Sophie's heart went out to the little creature. "What . . . what makes him cry so much?"

"No one loves . . . Boo-hoo!" the little Stone-Softener squeaked again, pressing himself against Sophie. She felt his hot tears seep through her jacket and jumped in alarm.

"Don't worry, he won't burn a hole through your skin," said Hammond. "The tears won't stain your jacket, either."

Sophie carefully stroked the soft fur again. Max reached and scratched the ghost between his ears, which looked like human ears, except that they were placed much higher on the head and had tufts of hair sprouting from them. Max's scratching appeared to calm the Stone-Softener. He relaxed, closed his eyes, and grunted softly.

"You're quite good at that," Hammond commented. "I knew that you were both quite talented! Can you watch him for a little longer? I have to look for an appropriate cage—one with walls not made of stone. At first, I put the little guy in a grotto. But he made a hole in the wall right away. If I hadn't been watching, he would have disappeared again."

Before Max or Sophie could reply, Hammond strode purposefully away. "He's in a hurry," mumbled Sophie. "I would have liked to ask him about the successor."

"Better not," said Max. "Then he'll know that we were snooping around his desk. I'm sure he'll tell us on his own. Should I take the Stone-Softener from you?"

"He's as light as air, but you can definitely hold him for a while if you want." Sophie carefully pried the furry arms from her neck and gently placed the ghost into Max's arms.

"Wow!" exclaimed Max. "He looks heavy, but he weighs practically nothing!"

"Boo-hoo isn't fat," howled the Stone-Softener as he began to drum on Max's shoulders with his fists. "Boo-hoo doesn't eat too much, not at all, not a bit . . ."

A few tears fell onto the gravel. It hissed, and Max and Sophie watched as they dissolved instantly. They were impressed. Hammond hadn't exaggerated.

"Is your name Boo-hoo?" Sophie asked, tickling the little ghost's nose. The ghost nodded and his blue eyes twinkled. "Boo-hoo is very, very old. And all alone."

"Poor thing," cooed Sophie.

"No one is nice to Boo-hoo," gulped the Stone-Softener and the tears flowed down his face in streams.

"But now we're here," said Max. "And aren't we

nice to you?"

The Stone-Softener looked at him. "Boo-hoo doesn't know," he whispered.

"Come on, we'll show you around," said Sophie. She was determined to distract the little ghost from his problems. Together they went to the cages with the pests. "Look at them, Boo-hoo."

As the Stone-Softener turned his head, a Snorting-with-Rage Ghost spit a stream of violet-colored slime into the middle of his face. Boo-hoo started howling again.

"Yuck, how mean!" cried Sophie. The Short-Tempered Ghost screeched with delight and the Snorting-with-Rage Ghost stuck out his tongue.

"We'll go somewhere else," Sophie huffed. "These pests are so annoying."

Max noticed Hammond's keys in the door of one of the pavilions.

"I know, let's go see Nelly and Nock," he suggested, and Sophie happily agreed.

But as they stepped into the room, they realized they had mixed up the pavilions. They weren't in the room with the aquarium; instead they were where the bottle and lamp genies were kept.

The Stone-Softener looked around curiously. "How awful . . . all locked up," he cried. "It's so tight . . . terrible, terrible, terrible!" His tears squirted onto the stone floor. Immediately countless holes were visible. They looked like the holes ladybugs make in the spring. It was as if swarms of bugs had crawled out of the floor!

"Let's get out of here!" cried Sophie. "Hammond will be mad when he sees the floor!" Quickly, they left the pavilion.

Neither Sophie nor Max had noticed that some tears had fallen onto an ancient-looking lamp. The ghost's tears immediately bore a hole in the lamp, and soon after, a cloud of smoke rose from the opening. The fog formed into a transparent figure wearing harem pants and a turban. It fell onto its knees and bowed deeply.

"I am Salabim," said the freed genie of the lamp. "At your service! Your wish is my command!" But as he stood up, he saw that he had thrown himself onto his knees before a glass case. There was no one for him to serve. Salabim was confused and angry at the same time. "And now what am I supposed to do? I'm a genie without a master." He grabbed the lamp and threw it to the floor. It broke into thousands of pieces. "Who am I supposed to serve?"

What now? Should he try to find his last mistress? He hadn't actually liked her very much. He had lived inside her pressed-powder compact, and because of that, his nose had constantly itched. More than once there had been problems because his mistress had to explain to curious people why her purse had just sneezed.

"No." Salabim shook his head. "I definitely won't go back to her. I'll just look for a new master or mistress—but first I will make sure I choose well." Satisfied with his decision, he nodded, disappeared in smoke, and slipped under the door into the open air.

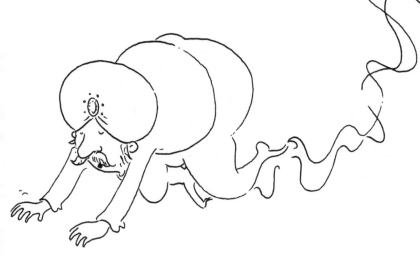

# Socks with Mayonnaise

In the meantime, Max and Sophie concerned themselves with the little Stone-Softener. Sophie had taken him into her arms again, and it was now up to her to calm him down.

"Be careful what you say," she whispered to Max. "He's so sensitive. One misplaced word and he'll start howling again." Max nodded. His little sister, Julia, was sometimes just the same.

Impatiently, they waited for Hammond's return. Finally, Hammond appeared in the distance on the gravel path. He was carrying, with some difficulty, a large wooden crate.

As he heaved it in front of the children with a sigh, a little puff of smoke slipped into Max's pocket. No one noticed it. Max felt something tickle his hip lightly, but he didn't pay any attention.

"I couldn't find anything better on such short notice," said Hammond. "This box will have to do for now."

"Boo-hoo wants a pretty home, not a box!" sniveled the Stone-Softener. "Boo-hoo wants a warm bed and a soft pillow . . . and Boo-hoo wants something to eat, too!"

"Of course, of course!" Hammond stroked his head softly. "But if you go into your crate now like a good little monster, I'll bring you your favorite thing to eat in just a moment."

Boo-hoo sighed. "Socks with mayonnaise." He rolled his eyes and licked his lips. His tongue was marked with black-and-white stripes. "Galoshes with red cabbage. Purses with whipped cream."

Sophie and Max exchanged looks and wrinkled their foreheads.

"Socks with mayonnaise—I think I can get you that, and later I'll bring you a pillow and a blanket," promised Hammond. Then, with the children's help, he carefully set Boo-hoo in the crate and carried the box into one of the pavilions.

"Whew!" sighed Hammond, when they were outside again. "That was quite a workout. Stone-Softeners are a little difficult to take care of. We've never had one before. I've heard a lot about them, but this is the first Stone-Softener that I've seen with my own eyes. A messenger from the Secret Council of 12 brought him this afternoon. He was captured in a nearby forest and was completely exhausted. I bet he has lived through something awful."

"He looks so adorable," said Sophie. "And if he wouldn't bawl all the time, I bet he would be a really great ghost."

Hammond agreed. "Stone-Softeners are lovely, but very needy creatures. Unfortunately, they tend to be very sad. Already several Stone-Softeners have drowned in puddles of their own tears. That's why there aren't very many left. They can actually live an incredibly long time." Hammond turned on his heel. "Let's go back to my office. I have to find some socks with mayonnaise as soon as possible so the little guy will trust me."

Max and Sophie followed him down the path. Both were disappointed. They had hoped to see more of Ghost Park today. They had still only seen a little bit of it.

"Are we going back through the Cerberus Catapult?" asked Sophie.

"This time we'll use the Toad's Temple," Hammond answered and turned left. Behind a shoulder-high hedge lay a pond filled with green water. It smelled like mildew. In the middle of the pond sat a large stone toad. It was almost completely overgrown with moss. Blood-red water lilies bloomed on the water's surface. Many of the flowers had not yet blossomed. But one opened just then with a clear "Ouch!"

Sophie jumped. "The water lilies are talking!" she cried.

"Yes?" asked Hammond. "What's so strange about that?" Without waiting for an answer, he knelt at the edge of the pond, dipped his arm in the water, and called out: "Wandering toads come to me! We are wanderers, all three."

The water bubbled, and then three large green toads marched in a line right up Hammond's arm. They came to a standstill and looked expectantly at him.

"What now?" asked Max weakly. He didn't like frogs or toads, although he liked most animals. But slimy creatures made him uneasy.

"Ick." Max made a face. Even Sophie was a little taken aback by the thought of a toad jumping on her face.

Hammond seemed surprised by their reaction. "Of course, there are other magical gates. But this method is the least dangerous. So let's go. Which one of you

will take the first toad?" He held one out with an open palm. "You're not going to chicken out, are you?"

Sophie definitely felt like a chicken. But she didn't want to appear like one in front of Max. Cautiously, she stretched out her right hand, grabbed the toad with her thumb and middle finger, and set it on her left arm.

The toad gazed at her. Its golden eyes glimmered as if they held a secret. Actually, this toad isn't so ugly, thought Sophie. His eyes are quite pretty.

*"Thank you. My name is Melusine, by the way."*

"And I'm Sophie," answered Sophie automatically. Then she caught herself. Who had spoken to her? Had the voice just been inside her head?

*"I'm a magical wandering toad, and I will gladly send you on your way, Sophie!"*

Squish! Something cool and damp had jumped onto her forehead. Although she had expected it, she was so startled that she took a large step backward, stumbled, and landed on her bottom. As she blinked she saw the castle ahead of her. She was sitting on the ground in the middle of some crocuses.

As she got to her feet, Max appeared beside her, his face carrying an expression of disgust and surprise, and soon after Hammond appeared, too.

"So, did I lie to you?" asked Hammond. "Pretty easy, right?"

"The toad," stuttered Sophie, who was still a little flustered, "she spoke to me. Her voice was suddenly in my head. She said that her name was Melusine." Sophie looked at Hammond. "Am I crazy or what? Did I imagine it all, or is that possible?"

"My toad didn't say anything to me," mumbled Max as he wiped his face. His toad had hopped onto his nose, and he felt as if it were still there.

"Melusine spoke with you?" asked Hammond, astounded. "That is quite an honor. A wandering toad will only speak to a few people! This just proves what I suspected after your experience with Mafalda—you have magic potential."

Sophie made a face. Magical skills? She wasn't sure if she wanted to have them or not. She would rather have mathematical skills. At least she could do something with those. Tomorrow she had to take a math test—and she was dreading it. She turned and followed Hammond into his office.

"Could you do me a favor?" asked the old man. "I don't actually think that I have mayonnaise or red cabbage in here. There's a supermarket a few blocks away. I only need enough for today and tomorrow. In the future, I'll just order it online with the other supplies. Certain items have to be specially ordered. Ghost delicacies like dried cockroaches, mandrake juice, mammoth meat, and snail jam. You can't get stuff like that at a normal supermarket." He turned the computer on, waited until it was ready, and then moved the mouse around. "Ah, there it is!"

Curious, Sophie and Max looked at the monitor. A photo of a thin young man popped up on screen. He had bushy eyebrows, a long narrow nose, and piercing eyes. His dark curly hair was shaggy and badly in need of a cut.

"Who is that?" asked Sophie.

"Jonathan von Fleuch," answered Hammond. "He is the son of the castle's owner who died, and he is the rightful heir to everything. We searched for him for a long time. Today, I finally received a letter from him."

Sophie held her breath and looked at Max.

"I had feared we would never find Jonathan." Hammond's voice sounded relieved. "Now I can finally turn over my responsibility for Ghost Park."

"Does that mean that we won't be needed anymore?" asked Max.

Hammond raised his head. "What will become of you? Hmm. Quite honestly, I hadn't thought of that at all. In the beginning, I'll have to train him, but after that, I don't know if he will need help."

Sophie pressed her lips together, and Max swallowed his disappointment. That certainly didn't sound reassuring!

But Hammond didn't seem to notice the children at all. Dreamily, he looked out the window. "Soon I'll be able to do what I love most: potting and planting. Then I won't have to struggle anymore with these creatures. Although some of them are quite nice, most of them are horrible plagues that should be locked up forever. I definitely would never have taken on this work of my own free will. But I gave my word of honor to the old owner on his deathbed. I promised I would take care of Ghost Park." His voice trailed off, and then he cleared his throat. "But that's another story." Abruptly, Hammond opened a drawer and pulled out some money, which he gave to Max and Sophie. "For the shopping."

Sophie had an idea. "My dad has lots of old socks in his closet. I can bring them along next time."

"And we still have galoshes in the garage that no one wears anymore," added Max.

"Great," replied Hammond. "But don't do anything that would make your parents ask questions. Because as you both know—discretion is of the utmost importance."

# The Ghost on the Toilet

"So I guess I'm broke again," mumbled Max. They had gone shopping and returned to the castle with the mayonnaise and cabbage. Now they were on their way home. "Once the heir shows up, we'll both be out of a job. And it was just starting to get exciting."

Sophie shrugged her shoulders. "Let's just wait and see. Maybe he will need our help after all." When they came to Max's street, Sophie waved and pedaled away. "Bye, see you at school tomorrow," she called.

When Max reached home, he found his father in the garage, busily hammering and sawing. The cage for the little bunny was almost finished. Only the front part was missing.

"It looks great," said Max. "Fluffy will definitely feel at home in there."

Mr. Hope grinned and took a step back to admire his work. "The little guy will be able to move in soon," he said, with more than a hint of pride in his voice.

Max's father would be able to build a great home for Boo-hoo. Too bad he wasn't allowed to say anything!

He turned and glanced around the garage. Sure enough, two pairs of ancient galoshes stood in one corner, completely dusty and full of spiderwebs. One pair was green, at least a size 13. The other pair had belonged to Max, but he had grown out of them long ago. He was sure that no one would miss the boots, and they would definitely make the Stone-Softener happy!

"I'll see you later," Max said to his father and went inside. He whistled on the steps, but as soon as his mother opened the door, he stopped. His mom was in a bad mood. He knew it the moment he looked at her.

"I thought we made it clear that your schoolwork couldn't suffer if you took this job," she said as she let him in.

"And it hasn't," answered Max.

"It doesn't look that way to me," said Mrs. Hope. "You've been gone all afternoon, and if I remember correctly, you have a math test tomorrow. When do you plan on studying for it?"

"But, Mom, I'm good at math," asserted Max. "I understand everything we're doing."

"I hope so." But his mother wasn't quite finished. She was looking at his pants. "I thought I told you on Saturday to throw your jeans in the wash. They're so dirty, they could stand on their own. You never pay attention to your clothes."

Max guessed that his mom was actually angry with his dad. Still that wasn't any reason to take it out on him! And besides, he thought the new rabbit's cage was great. His dad was really good at stuff like that, and it wasn't his fault that other people didn't appreciate his talents.

"Go wash your hands," said his mom. "And make

sure you clean up the sink after you're finished."

Max headed into the bathroom, washed his hands, and stuffed his dirty jeans into the hamper, just like his mom had asked.

"Ouch!" Max jumped. Was he hallucinating? In Ghost Park, the water lilies had said ouch, but until now his pants had never spoken to him. The idea made him grin. He imagined his mother's face if the jeans were to say to her, "Please wash me!" Or if they yelled while being ironed: "Ouch! Ouch! Too hot!"

He'd have to remember that one. Maybe he could even make a good bedtime story out of it for Julia. Laughing to himself, Max left the bathroom. He had barely closed the door when a puff of smoke rose through a crack in the hamper and transformed into a figure in harem pants and a turban.

"Now where am I?" Salabim asked, gazing around. He sniffed the shower curtain, licked the soap, and tentatively bit into the bath sponge. Disgusted, he put it back. Then he tried out the tub's faucet, but pulled away as a spurt of hot water shot out of the pipe. "Ouch!" He quickly shut the faucet off and blew on his tender hands. Then he turned to examine the counter next to the sink. There were so many tubes and little containers. What was all this stuff for? Maybe one of the containers would be a nice place to sleep tonight? Salabim lifted the top of Mrs. Hope's night cream, sniffed Julia's bubble bath, and unscrewed the cap of the toothpaste. He liked the peppermint aroma and inhaled deeply.

"Mmmm, that smells so good!" he said. "It reminds me of my homeland and the bazaars with their countless spices! Let's just see what it looks like on the inside." In a cloud of smoke, Salabim vanished and slipped into the tube of toothpaste.

He had barely disappeared when Mrs. Hope came into the bathroom and threw Julia's gym clothes into the hamper. She admired the sink, which Max had actually left clean. But then she noticed the uncapped tube of toothpaste.

"Typical Julia," she mumbled, screwing the cap back on.

During dinner, Mr. Hope couldn't stop yawning. Although his work on the rabbit stall had been a lot of fun, it had also been exhausting. He had been busy the entire day. He gave short answers whenever his wife or children asked him a question. Julia, however, couldn't keep her mouth shut. Excitedly, she explained how she had burrowed through some bushes and stumbled across a hedgehog at preschool.

"He was hibernating and was just as tired as Daddy," she announced happily.

Mr. Hope stood up from the table. "I think I'll go to bed early tonight. My throat is scratchy. I might be getting a cold."

In the bathroom, Mr. Hope first reached for the tweezers to pull a splinter from his finger. Then he unscrewed the cap of the children's toothpaste without realizing it and gave it a squeeze.

"Owww!"

Mr. Hope stared at the tube in dismay. Had the cry come from inside? As he nervously peered into the end of the tube, a bunch of toothpaste shot from the opening and squirted directly onto his face. Mr. Hope screamed and dropped the tube into the sink.

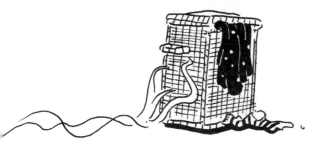

Worriedly, Mrs. Hope ran to the bathroom. "What happened? Did you slip? You screamed!"

Mr. Hope turned to look at her, his face covered with toothpaste.

"Oh, my goodness!" Mrs. Hope couldn't suppress her smile. She handed him a towel. "Something like that could only happen to you!"

"I couldn't help it," said Mr. Hope. "The toothpaste just squirted out! I didn't even squeeze that hard." He rinsed the toothpaste from his face and dried it. He had really had enough for one day. All he wanted now was to go to bed.

As soon as Mr. Hope left the bathroom, smoke seeped out of the toothpaste tube, and Salabim appeared.

"That wasn't the right master for me," he sighed. Deep in thought, he sat on the toilet seat, holding his head in his hands. "Oh, if only I could find the right someone to serve. I would fulfill their every wish. I would do everything that was in my power to make him or her happy . . ." He sighed again.

Then he heard footsteps. He looked up and saw the handle on the door moving. Oh, no—it was too late to slip back into the tube!

Julia came in. She marched purposefully to the sink, grabbed her toothbrush, and started reaching for the toothpaste.

Salabim took a deep breath. "Just imagine that you had three wishes—what would you wish for, young lady?"

Julia whirled around. Her eyes grew as big as saucers as she looked at Salabim. "Who are you?" she whispered.

"I am Salabim, Genie of the Lamp," he answered, bowing so deeply that his turban slipped off his head and rolled in front of Julia's feet. "But, at this time, I am currently without a lamp or a master or, in your case, a mistress. But I hope that will all change very soon."

Julia stared at the turban and dropped her toothbrush. "HELP! HELP!" Screaming, she ran out of the bathroom, down the hallway, and into her mother's arms. "A ghost is sitting on the toilet!" she howled. "I'm serious. And he asked what I wanted to wish for . . ."

"Calm down, Julia." Her mom hugged her tightly. "That was just Dad with lots of toothpaste on his face."

Adamant, Julia pulled away. "But I know what Daddy looks like!" She stomped her feet. "And that wasn't him. It was a real ghost and it had—"

"What about me?" Her dad's voice drifted out of the half-open bedroom door. "I'm in here."

"It was a real ghost," proclaimed Julia once more. "He said that I had three wishes, and then his turban fell off and rolled in front of my feet."

Pale-faced, Max came out of the kitchen. He had heard everything that Julia had said. Clearly, she was telling the truth. Something had gone very wrong.

"What?" he asked her. "Did you say that a ghost is sitting on our toilet?"

His mother's eyes flashed with anger. "Yes, just listen to her! You're the one putting all that nonsense into her head. You are always telling her ghost stories. It's no wonder she's starting to see ghosts everywhere!"

"But it's true," squeaked Julia. "I really saw the ghost, honestly!"

"I'll take care of this," said Max, and he slipped into the bathroom before anyone else could go in. He closed the door and locked it. Then he turned around, determined to set things straight with the ghost.

Salabim bowed. "Greetings, Master." Max felt his knees grow weak. He had counted on a little ghost, at the most just a poltergeist. Something about the size of the Stone-Softener. But this guy was bigger than

his dad. It occurred to Max how little experience he actually had with ghosts. How did you know whether a ghost was dangerous?

"What do you want?" Max didn't want to let the ghost know how scared he was. He had to be brave and decidedly bold.

"What do I want?" repeated the ghost. "It's better if you tell me what you want. Then I can fulfill three wishes." Thoughts whirled around inside Max's head. He tried to remember everything he had read about situations like this. There were ghosts that were friendly at first but later turned bad. Max knew he had to be careful.

141

"Oh, the number with the three wishes," he said and tried to make his voice sound casual. "That's so old. Can't you think of something new?"

The ghost was taken aback. "So I shouldn't grant you three wishes?"

"Just one," said Max. "Go back where you came from."

"Your wish is my command." Immediately, the ghost turned into a cloud of smoke.

Max had thought the ghost would go back to Ghost Park. But he was utterly surprised to see the cloud of smoke sneaking into the tube of toothpaste. Without hesitating, he screwed the cap back on. Now the ghost was caught! Max's heart was beating like a drum. It had gone well this time! The ghost certainly could've torn him into tiny pieces if he had wanted to.

His mom knocked on the bathroom door. "Why did you lock yourself in, Max? What are you doing in there? Come on, open up!"

Max took a deep breath. "Just a second." Quickly he stuck the tube of toothpaste in his pocket. Better safe than sorry! Under no circumstance should Julia be allowed to have the tube again. Then he turned the lock. His mom and Julia stepped inside the room. Mrs. Hope looked searchingly around the room. "You see, it's exactly like I said. No ghost. Nothing. Not even the tiniest of ghosts. You were dreaming, Julia."

"I wasn't," persisted Julia. She looked at Max. "What did you do with him?"

"Flushed him down the toilet," replied Max.

"Really?"

"I had to flush three times until he finally went down the drain," Max replied with a serious expression.

"Just stop it, Max!" Mrs. Hope cried. "I really can't stand it anymore, and you are starting to scare Julia. Now look, Julia, the ghost is gone. Disappeared. Vanished into thin air. Now you can brush your teeth and go to bed."

Julia nodded. While his mom was busy with Julia, Max retreated to his bedroom. He looked for a good hiding place for the toothpaste. But nothing seemed secure enough. Finally, he put it in his backpack. It was highly unlikely that his mother or Julia would look in there. Then he heard Julia in the bathroom, whining for her special toothpaste.

"Your dad must have thrown it away," was his mother's answer. "Don't be so picky, Julia. Here, use ours for tonight."

Max sighed deeply and fell backward onto his bed. He would have liked to call Sophie and talk with her, but it was late. He would have to wait until tomorrow. What a day!

# A Trap for Max and Sophie

As Mr. Kern collected the math tests, Max had a bad feeling. He had definitely not done well this time! He hadn't had the slightest clue how to solve two of the four problems. And he wasn't even sure if the answers for the two he *had* understood were correct.

He could already imagine the lecture he was going to get from his mom. Recently, she had become a lot more serious about Max's grades.

Max glanced at Sophie out of the corner of his eyes. She was making the same pitiful face that he was. Apparently, her test had gone just as poorly as his. He sighed. It seemed silly, but he just hadn't been able to concentrate. The whole time he had been thinking of the ghost—the ghost he had trapped in the toothpaste tube and who was now in his backpack. How had the ghost succeeded in escaping and coming home with Max? Would Hammond have an answer for him? Finally, the bell rang.

As Sophie started to leave the classroom with a pair of her friends, Max tugged on her sleeve. "I have to talk to you."

"What's up?" asked Sophie.

"I can only tell you when we're totally alone."

Vicky and Nicole nudged one another and exchanged understanding looks.

"Maybe he wants to tell you he *loves* you," said Vicky.

"Oh, be quiet," hissed Sophie. "You guys go on ahead, I'll catch up." When they were alone Sophie sat on Max's desk. "Shoot."

Max pulled the tube of toothpaste out of his bag. "There is a ghost in here." He told Sophie the crazy story about what had happened the night before at the Hope's house.

"The ghost definitely escaped from Ghost Park," said Sophie. "Yesterday when we were in the pavilion with the bottle and lamp genies, I guess we must have inadvertently let one out."

Max nodded. "That's what I thought, too."

Sophie grinned. "Why didn't you set him free during the math quiz? That would have improved things in the classroom a little bit."

Max grinned, too, but then turned serious. "I don't trust myself enough to let him out," he said decidedly. "He's really big and if he were ever in a bad mood . . ."

Sophie agreed. "Better safe than sorry. Maybe it's best if we just ask Hammond for advice."

As soon as he finished speaking a teacher stuck his head in the room. "What, you're not outside?" There was a rule that every student must exit the building during recesses. The rule even applied on rainy days, but whether it was enforced or not depended on which teacher was on duty. Some teachers just looked the

145

other way. But today the sun was shining, and the teacher on duty was one of the stricter ones.

"Outside," he commanded, pointing at the door.

"We have blackboard duty," lied Sophie. She slid off the desk, grabbed a sponge, and started cleaning the blackboard.

The teacher wrinkled his forehead. This was certainly not the first time he had heard this excuse. Max went to help Sophie and grabbed a cloth in order to dry the board. The teacher watched them for a while.

"Just don't forget to go outside when you're done," he said. Then he spotted the toothpaste on Max's desk and, before they could stop him, he held it in his hand.

"What is toothpaste doing here?"

"That's mine," said Sophie as quick as lightning. She had been blessed with the most naturally perfect teeth.

"I brush my teeth after every meal."

Max was again impressed by her skill. He exhaled as the teacher laid the tube back down.

"If either of you are planning some sort of prank with this . . ." The teacher raised a finger in warning and left the room.

Sophie exhaled and laid down the sponge. "Thank goodness! I just about had a heart attack."

"Me, too." Max swallowed hard. "He didn't have the slightest idea how bad a prank we could pull with this! But then again I guess it wouldn't have to be a prank," he said dreamily. If the genie could fulfill every wish, Max would be so powerful! How easy his life would be. He wouldn't have any more problems. He would always have enough allowance, his father would get a great job, and he definitely wouldn't have to worry about school anymore.

Sophie handed him the tube and gave him a warning look. "It might be really dangerous. And Hammond would definitely be very disappointed in us."

Max sighed and put the toothpaste in his jacket pocket. "You're right. Unfortunately. It was just a thought anyway."

"Oh, Max," said Sophie. "Do you know how often I've wished for my own math genie? You know, a little tiny genie who could whisper the right answers in my ear?" She made a face. "Now I'm definitely getting a tutor. My parents have been threatening that for a while. They want me to take over their dental practice when I'm older, and to get into dental college, I have to do super well in school."

"Poor thing," said Max sympathetically. Sometimes parents were more difficult than ghosts!

At three that afternoon Sophie and Max once again stood in front of the castle. Max had brought the old galoshes from the garage and Sophie had a bag filled with discarded socks.

"There'll be a feast for Boo-hoo," said Sophie happily as she lifted her gift out of her bike's basket.

"Hopefully, he hasn't spoiled his appetite," said Max. "I wonder if he'll eat it all in one go?"

"I have no idea how greedy little Stone-Softeners are," answered Sophie.

Hammond wasn't in his office again. This time Sophie and Max didn't look for him for very long in the normal park. They went immediately to the poplar trees and to the Alley of Dreams, where they both had the same nightmare: Mr. Kern handed back their math tests—and they both had big fat **F**'s!

They were both a little dazed as they walked down the alley toward the circular flower bed and the pavilions. The door to one of the pavilions was open. Sophie and Max were sure that Hammond would be there. But as they stepped into the room, they were surprised to discover a stranger. He was standing over an aquarium, his back to them, and he was trying to catch the little mermaid! Nelly was swimming frantically back and forth. The tiny merman Nock tried to come to her rescue, angrily stabbing the stranger in the hand with his trident. But soon the stranger had forced the mermaid into a corner, and she could no longer escape. He was about to snatch her up, when Sophie screamed, "What are you doing?"

The stranger whirled around. The merman took the opportunity to aim his trident well. With a scream, the man pulled his hand out of the aquarium, and Nelly was free. Within seconds, the tiny creatures dove under the water, murky from all the turmoil.

"Who are you and how did you get here?" the stranger bellowed.

"We could ask you the same question," countered Sophie. But she already knew who the stranger was. His features looked familiar to her. He had to be the man she and Max had seen on Hammond's computer yesterday:

Jonathan von Fleuch, the heir to the castle and its grounds.

"How many people know about the secret of Ghost Park if even children are wandering in?" snarled the stranger. He looked as if he were about to explode.

Sophie felt her knees go weak. What a repulsive man! How heartlessly he had gone after Nelly!

"No one knows anything," replied Max. "Didn't Mr. Hammond tell you about us? We're his assistants."

Sophie waited for the stranger's reply. On the one hand, she was relieved that Max had explained everything. On the other hand, she was surprised that he was talking so freely with the stranger. Didn't he find the man just as repulsive as she did? She didn't want to talk to him at all!

"Ahhhh, Hammond," the man said thoughtfully. "He didn't tell me anything about any assistants."

Max glanced at Sophie worriedly. But she didn't notice because she was studying the heir. The man was tall and gaunt, and he wore a coarsely knit gray sweater and black corduroys. Sophie noticed that the left cuff of his pants was checked instead of black as if the tailor had run out of fabric. And his shoes didn't match. They were both made out of black leather, but the left shoe was covered with tiny holes and the right shoe had none. How strange!

"You can ask Mr. Hammond all about it," said Max. "The SCT allowed him to hire two assistants—and that's us."

Sophie noticed how the stranger listened more

closely as Max mentioned the Secret Council of 12.

"So, you both already know about the SCT?" he asked slowly. "Very interesting, very interesting! Hammond apparently squealed about everything!"

Now Sophie decided that she definitely did not want to work with this man. He was very unpleasant.

"Mr. Hammond will be able to explain everything," said Max.

"Yes, as he should. I will demand that he will." The stranger touched Max's shoulder. "Come, my young friend, we'll go to see him now."

Sophie wanted to pull Max back—just as she had done in front of Mafalda. But she caught herself. She shouldn't show her dislike for the man so clearly. The stranger started to leave the pavilion with Max in tow.

"What about me?" she called.

At first, the arrogant man seemed to look right through her! Then he pointed a finger at her. "You wait here . . . and watch out."

"Watch out?" Sophie raised her eyebrows. "For what?"

"Well, for everything." Then he and Max disappeared.

Sophie glanced about uneasily. She didn't have a good feeling about this. But maybe she was just worrying too much. Hammond would definitely be able to explain everything. Maybe it would all work out, and the heir would accept her and be a little nicer to her. But deep inside, she didn't believe it at all.

To distract herself, she carefully approached the

aquarium. The water was still murky. Nelly and Nock were hiding. Sophie remembered the enchanting scene the first time she had visited Ghost Park. The little mermaid had sat on the aquarium's edge and combed her long hair while humming to herself. The merman had lovingly given her a kiss.

"Poor Nelly, poor Nock," murmured Sophie. "You disliked that nasty man just as much as I do, right?" A few bubbles rose to the water's surface, but Sophie had no idea if they had heard her or not.

"Hammond is in his office," Jonathan von Fleuch said to Max. "We'll take the Cerberus Catapult."

"No, he's not in his office," replied Max. "We were just there and didn't see him."

The heir gave Max a look that chilled him to the bone. "When I say something, you better believe me. HAMMOND IS THERE." Something in his voice told Max that it was probably a good idea to keep his mouth shut.

Max shrugged his shoulders. Well, fine, if the heir insisted. He would see shortly that the old man was not there.

The huge dog's mouth, camouflaged against a cliff, looked even bigger and scarier to Max than the first time. It took a lot of courage to step inside with Jonathan beside him. The heir noticed Max's hesitation. "Are you afraid?" he teased. "Or are you just scared of me?"

Max shook his head, although he felt extremely uncomfortable. He had already taken the Cerberus

Catapult once to get back to the castle. Why wouldn't it would work a second time?

Carefully, Max set his foot on the slippery tongue and balanced himself as he walked deeper into the mouth.

"It would be best if *you* tickled the uvula," said Jonathan. "I have some problems with my shoulder joints and I can't reach up very well."

Obediently, Max stretched upward. His hand had almost reached the slimy uvula when he was pushed from behind! He lost his balance, fell forward, and slipped into the throat. As he slid into the darkness, Max heard Jonathan's laughter behind him. "THAT'S WHAT WE DO WITH OUR ASSISTANTS!" the heir yelled.

Max began to scream as he slid deeper and deeper. Colors flew past him, red and violet, blue and green.

Hadn't Hammond warned not to go near the throat?

*"You'll land in a deeply magical realm . . ."*

Now, what did that mean? Would he ever be able to get out? Max was close to fainting as he landed with a plop on something soft.

* * * GP * * *

Meanwhile, Sophie discovered that Max had left his bag of galoshes in the pavilion. She decided to look for the Stone-Softener on her own. Hammond must have left him somewhere nearby. She took the bags and left the pavilion. The Snorting-with-Rage Ghosts and Poison-Spitters hung on the bars of their cages, but didn't make as much noise as usual. Sophie thought they looked hungry. The little ghosts followed her every move. As she walked past them they looked at her, decidedly disappointed.

Sophie felt like she should apologize to them. "I don't know what Hammond feeds you," she said. "I'm sure he'll be coming back soon and will bring you something." Did the pests understand what she was saying? Sophie wasn't sure. Then she saw Hammond walking toward her. Relieved, she ran up to him.

"I'm so glad you're here!" she blurted. "We've been looking for you. Max went away with that strange man. Can you imagine—he almost caught the little mermaid!" Finally, she stopped to take a breath.

"Well," said Hammond slowly. "That wasn't very nice of him . . ."

Sophie stopped abruptly. Hammond seemed different. He looked like he always did, but his friendly smile was missing. Even the expression in his eyes was different. Then Sophie noticed that his green gardening pants were checked at the bottom of his left leg. And one of Hammond's shoes was covered with tiny holes!

"Something's not right . . ." stammered Sophie, and she took a step back. "You're not Mr. Hammond."

"That's right, you little lizard," said Hammond, as his face twisted with anger. "You are extremely bothersome, do you know that? Curious little monsters like you should be locked up. Hear that? LOCKED UP!"

Sophie stared in disbelief as Hammond pulled out some yellowed pages from his pocket and hastily read over them. In seconds, he had found what he was looking for. He stretched out his hand as he began to recite:

*Stone for stone*
*and rock for rock.*
*Keep her imprisoned*
*around the clock!*

"NO!" screamed Sophie.

But Hammond had barely finished speaking when stones appeared from all directions, flying directly toward her. Sophie ducked to shield herself from the rain of stones, but they fell on the ground around her. In no time they had formed a ring at her feet and then a wall that grew higher and higher. In disbelief, Sophie watched as the wall quickly rose past her knees, then her hips, and finally her head. She was trapped on all sides, and then the rocks built a roof over her head.

"I don't want to be left here," screamed Sophie and pounded against the walls. But it was useless. The stones would not budge. And it became darker and darker around her as the roof filled in over her head. "I WANT OUT!"

"Sure, that will happen on the same day that all your other dreams come true," came the monotone answer from the fake Hammond. Sophie heard him laughing gleefully at her predicament.

Now the magical prison was finished. It was dark inside except for a tiny hole in the middle of the roof. Sophie squinted up at the hole, then covered her face with her hands, and began to cry.

# Ghosts to the Rescue

Max looked around and tried to recover from the shock of falling. He had landed as softly as if he had fallen onto a sand dune on the beach. In front of him lapped a glittering dark sea. Max stared at the water and swallowed hard. He had just been in a large mouth and then had slipped down into a throat. If his knowledge of biology was correct, he must be in a stomach. He had to force himself not to think of stomach acid.

All he saw above him was darkness with a few colorful lights that brightened and then darkened like a muted fireworks display. Now and then a few rainbow-colored shooting stars sizzled overhead. Were they some sort of chemical reaction? Or just magic illuminations? Max pondered both options.

Then he remembered what Hammond had said as he explained the Cerberus Catapult—you shouldn't despair if you slipped down into the throat and landed in one of the deeply magical realms. You could be retrieved eventually. Hammond would just have to notify the Secret Council of 12. "But to do that, Hammond has to know that I'm here," mumbled Max. How could he get that message to him? And what was happening to Sophie? She would definitely start to worry if he was away too long!

Max put his head in his hands. What could he do now? Suddenly he remembered the tube of toothpaste and the genie inside. Was the tube still in his jacket pocket? Yes—there it was! Maybe the ghost could help him—or destroy him. But he had to take the risk. With trembling fingers, he unscrewed the cap.

"Genie, come out!" His voice broke with excitement. A thread of smoke rose from the tube, growing thicker and larger until it formed a figure in a turban and harem pants. The ghost fell to its knees before Max.

"I am Salabim, your obedient servant."

Max hesitated. He wasn't used to having someone kneel so submissively before him. Was it just a trick?

"Don't you want to break my neck?" asked Max distrustfully.

"Well, if that's what you wish. But that would be

too bad." Salabim raised his eyes toward Max, and Max looked directly into his round, good-natured face. It seemed that the genie was speaking in earnest.

"No, it's not what I want. Stand up," commanded Max. "What I want is to get out of here. Can you do that?"

The ghost raised himself off the ground and looked around. "You're right, my good man, it's not particularly comfortable here. Where are we, actually?"

"It's quite possible that we're in Cerberus's stomach."

"Oh, no! How did that happen?"

"I was shoved," Max told the genie. "The man who inherited Ghost Park is awful. He intentionally pushed me."

"Oh, no!" repeated the ghost. He leaned his head back and looked up. "It goes on for quite a while, young man. I cannot see the end."

Max nodded. "Well, I fell for quite a while. Do you think you can do it?"

"We can try." The genie took off his turban, unrolled it, and spread the cloth out onto the ground. "Have a seat, sir."

"Huh?" Max gaped. "Why do you want me to sit there?"

"Sir, I know it is a little small, but unfortunately I cannot offer you a flying carpet," answered Salabim with an obsequious bow.

"You mean . . . this thing . . . flies?" stammered Max.

"But of course!"

Max hesitated, then sat down on the cloth. The ghost took a seat beside him, stretched out his arms, and quietly began to murmur a spell.

Max grabbed his arm. "Wait, stop a minute. I think I'm still a little dizzy."

"Then just close your eyes." Salabim stretched out his arms once more and chanted:

> *Gravity, dear turban, defy.*
> *Lift off the ground and fly.*
> *Most of the day, I carry you;*
> *Now to my command*
> *Listen true.*
> *Upward you will soar,*
> *Away from the floor,*
> *I'll take care of the guest*
> *While you do the rest.*

Nothing happened. The cloth didn't budge.

"Darn it," said Salabim. "It won't go. Normally it lifts off when I say soar."

"Maybe I'm too heavy," suggested Max.

"I doubt it. I've already flown on this with an elephant."

"Honestly?" Max looked at Salabim in disbelief.

"Well, yes, but it was a little elephant. His name was Pick-Nick, and he was my daughter's favorite elephant. I gave him to her for her birthday."

"You have a daughter?" Max asked in surprise.

"What, genies aren't supposed to have families?"

160

asked Salabim. "Of course I have a daughter. Liliette the Beautiful. Far and wide, she was the prettiest girl until an evil genie turned her into a cactus."

"Oh," said Max, dismayed. "I'm very sorry."

Salabim wiped a furtive tear from his cheek. "One day I'm going to find that cactus, I know that much for sure. But for now, let's think about how we're going to get out of here. Since it's not working with the turban, I bet the air here is full of magic and my little cloth isn't strong enough."

"Can't you magically pull a ladder or something out of thin air?" suggested Max.

"I'm not exactly good with magic, sir," said Salabim softly. "It's a little embarrassing for me to admit this, but when I was young, I received very poor grades in magic class, because I was too lazy to learn the spells. Besides that, I generally skipped four out of five classes.

But I have always looked out for the well-being of my masters. For example, I can make it smell like lemons in here, or lull you to sleep and give you the most pleasant dreams . . . And if I have the right ingredients I'm actually quite an accomplished chef."

He can't do magic, thought Max. Disappointment engulfed him. "But then why did you say you could grant me three wishes?"

"Well, there are wishes for which very little magic is needed," answered Salabim. "It might be that you wish for the air to smell like lemons or that you wish for a nap—"

"NO!" shouted Max. "I don't want to smell LEMONS, I want to get out of here, do you UNDER-STAND?"

"Yes," said Salabim. "You needn't shout. I can understand you perfectly well when you speak to me normally."

Just then something bubbled in the sea. Was Max imagining it or was the water coming nearer? What would happen when it came over the banks? And if this really was stomach acid . . . were they about to be DIGESTED?

"I hope something occurs to you soon, in fact, right away!" Max said, gazing fearfully at the sea.

"Is that your wish?"

"Yes."

"Hm . . ." Salabim rolled his turban up and placed it back on top of his head. Then he touched his finger to the tip of his nose. After a few seconds he called out:

"I've got it!"

"Let's hear it," said Max, feeling suddenly tired.

"Can you disappear in smoke?"

"Of course not."

"That's too bad, then that won't work either," mumbled Salabim and was again silent.

"What was your plan?" asked Max.

"We could've both changed into smoke and drifted upward," said Salabim. "Without a ladder and without a flying turban."

Suddenly, an idea popped into Max's head. "That's what you should do! You change into smoke and go get help." He practically sparkled with excitement. "You have to tell Hammond where I am. And please tell Sophie, too." He thought about this for a second, then added: "But also tell her not to worry about me." He glanced at the sea, which had moved even closer. "I'm fine. At least for now."

Salabim shook his head. "That plan might work, but, unfortunately, there is a problem, sir."

"What?"

"Now that I've found a master I'm not supposed to leave him!" Salabim was indignant. "It's out of the question!"

Max took a deep breath. "WHAT IF I COMMAND YOU TO GO AND GET HELP?"

The genie sighed, clearly tormented. "I guess then I must do it. But you mustn't always be so strict. Goodbye, see you soon." He turned into smoke and rose upward.

Max watched him until there was nothing more to see. Then he squatted on the ground. "I hope he hurries," he mumbled to himself, and stared at the sinister sea.

* * * GP * * *

Salabim did not like the Cerberus Catapult. First of all, such a magical gate was supposed to keep ghosts from escaping from Ghost Park into the human world. Normally ghosts couldn't use the Cerberus Catapult—at least not without a human accompanying them. And if ghosts tried to leave without a human companion then the giant mouth closed, the teeth began to chew, and the poor ghosts were so traumatized that all thoughts of fleeing left their heads. Then, after a while, the huge mouth opened again and the ghost was free—at least to go back into Ghost Park.

Salabim rose as a wisp of smoke through the throat. It was a long way up, similar to a tall chimney.

"Does this ever end?" muttered Salabim. Finally, he could see a light shimmering in the distance. He slid by the uvula and regained his true form. Just as he realized he was already in the large mouth—to his left and right were huge craggy teeth—the dog's mouth snapped shut and it was suddenly pitch-black.

The ground began to shake. Salabim lost his balance. He fell onto the tongue and rolled back and forth until it occurred to him to hold tightly onto one of the teeth.

"ESCAPING IS NOT ALLOWED!" a dark voice in his

head warned him. Cerberus was speaking to him!

"I don't want to escape," Salabim called out in confusion, while being shaken hard the entire time.

"THAT'S WHAT THEY ALL SAY!"

"But it's true, really," protested the genie. "I must rescue my master . . . let me go!"

"ONLY AFTER I HAVE TAUGHT YOU A LESSON!" The shaking grew even worse.

"Oh, no, no, no, no!" begged Salabim. "Why must you do that? I'm just a lowly genie, trying to serve his master . . ." Finally, the mouth opened.

Salabim crawled into the open air. He was so dizzy he didn't even try to stand. He was also nauseous. "What did I do to deserve that?" he whined. "Oh, how nice it was before in the lady's compact!" He took a few deep breaths. Slowly he felt better. The fresh air helped. At last he could stand. Then he immediately remembered his task. Max had commanded him to tell Hammond and Sophie the news. But where were they? Salabim decided to turn himself into smoke once more. As a cloud in the sky he would have the best view.

Sophie was already hoarse from yelling so much. But so far, no one had answered her cries for help. Disheartened, Sophie sat on the floor in her stone prison. How was she ever going to get out of here? She had already tested every point in the wall for weaknesses. She had tried to climb toward the little opening in the roof, but had only succeeded in scraping her knees. She had even tried tying the old socks together and making a rope, but it hadn't worked.

"I'm never going to get out of here!" she groaned. "I'm just going to die of hunger or thirst." Tears ran down her cheeks again. She wiped them away. She had already cried so much, but of course it hadn't helped. Neither had yelling. She decided to try calling out just once more. She cupped her hands around her mouth and took a deep breath. "HELP!" she screamed with all her might. "MAX, WHERE ARE YOU? CAN ANYONE HEAR ME?"

And this time someone did hear her. Salabim had been floating as a small cloud over Ghost Park. He hadn't found Hammond anywhere. There was only a

stranger walking around the park. Salabim decided
to ask him for help and slowly sank toward the ground.
He was just about to change his shape when he caught
a whiff of the stranger. Salabim had an extremely sensitive nose. It was the one thing he could always count
on. He could even smell when something evil was
afoot. AND HE SMELLED IT NOW! It stank so much
that Salabim held his nose and turned quickly back
into a puff of smoke. He didn't want anything to do
with such a man! He was definitely not friendly!

The stranger looked up as he heard sneezing. But
he only saw a little harmless cloud hanging in the sky.

The stranger shrugged his shoulders and went on. The cloud hurried in the other direction. Whew! thought Salabim. That was definitely the man who had shoved Max. I have to stay away from him! He's definitely up to no good!

He remembered the evil genie who had turned his daughter into a cactus. He had smelled just as bad! Stop! What was that? Had someone called out? Salabim searched the ground below. He saw a small building that looked like a large stone egg.

"CAN ANYONE HEAR ME?"

It was a girl's voice! It had to be Sophie.

The cloud descended toward the stone egg. Salabim discovered an opening in the roof, turned into a wisp of smoke, and slid inside.

Sophie was taken aback as Salabim suddenly assumed his genie form in front of her.

"Wh-wh-who are y-y-you?" Sophie cried.

"I am Salabim," answered the ghost with a deep bow. "Have no fear. I bring you greetings from my master. You are not to worry, he is doing well . . ."

Sophie swallowed. She remembered what Max had told her earlier that afternoon. "Are you the genie from the toothpaste tube?"

"Exactly," said Salabim. "But the tube was just my temporary home. Normally, I live in lamps."

"Where is Max?" blurted Sophie. Her nerves were frayed, and she couldn't stand to hear a long explanation. "He's supposed to get me out of here, right away!" She hiccupped.

"Unfortunately he can't," Salabim said regretfully.

"Why not?"

"Because Max is waiting for someone to get him out, too."

"Oh, no." Sophie stared at the ghost. "What happened to him?"

Salabim told her everything he knew.

Sophie chewed on her lip. It sounded so terrible!

"Hammond has to help us," she said. "He has to alert the Secret Council of 12 right away!"

"Unfortunately, I was unable to find Hammond anywhere," said Salabim. "I only saw that other man." He held his nose to show Sophie his disdain for the man. "He smelled awful!"

"Smelled?" asked Sophie.

"Yes," insisted Salabim. "And that means that he's up to no good."

"I'm not surprised," Sophie said dully. "He shoved Max into the deeply magical realm and had this wall built around me."

"Hmm." Salabim put his finger to his nose, as he did whenever he needed to consider something carefully. "Could it be that he has also somehow gotten Ham-

mond out of the way?"

"Definitely," said Sophie. "So I have to notify the Secret Council of 12. Come on, get me out of here."

"Oh," said Salabim sheepishly. "If I only could, but unfortunately, I cannot."

"You cannot?" asked Sophie, flabbergasted. "Why can't you just magically whisk the wall away? Genies can normally fulfill any wish, right?"

"Not all of them."

"Oh."

"I know you are terribly disappointed," said the genie. "I am very sorry. If I had known, I wouldn't have made such a fool out of myself. I would have done better in school and done all of my homework assignments; I never would have skipped a single class and—"

"Oh, just be quiet," said Sophie, annoyed. "I have

to think this over. I'll come up with something eventually."

Salabim squatted next to her and was quiet. "Are
you still thinking?" he asked after a while.

"Uh, yes."

The ghost twiddled his thumbs and counted to ten—
twice.

"Is this going to take a while?" he asked.

"YESSS!"

"I just mean, um, that Max is waiting . . ."

All of a sudden Sophie threw the sack with the old
socks at him. As soon as she had done it she was sorry.
"I'm sorry. But if you keep interrupting me I can't
concentrate."

Salabim wasn't offended. Curious, he stuck his nose
in the bag. "What are those for?"

"Oh—those are just old socks. They are food for
Boo-hoo . . ." Sophie stopped. The Stone-Softener!

Instantly, a plan formed in her mind. Salabim had to
free the Stone-Softener from his cage and bring him to
her. When Boo-hoo heard about what had happened to
her and Max he would surely start weeping—and his
tears would burn holes in Sophie's prison. That was the
solution!

Sophie jumped up. "You won't believe it, Salabim,
but we can do it without magic!"

The ghost listened to her plan and a wide grin spread
across his face.

"You are almost as smart as my daughter . . . and she
was the smartest girl under the sun!"

"Don't waste time flattering me, Mr. Genie of the Lamp. Just get to work!"

And Salabim really did hurry. He freed the Stone-Softener from his cage and carried him to the stone egg, all the while being careful not to encounter the stranger. When Boo-hoo heard what had happened he cried and cried, his tears flowing like water, and, in no time, they had bored a hole in the wall. Sophie was free in minutes. She hugged and kissed the little Stone-Softener, who immediately tore into the old socks.

"Too dry!" he complained at once and disappointedly spit out a piece of sock. "Boo-hoo wants mayonnaise!"

"We'll get some in the castle," Sophie promised. "There is a ton of it in Hammond's office—we bought some yesterday." Boo-hoo beamed as she took him into her arms. "But first we have to go through the Cerberus Catapult."

Salabim made a face. "I think you should know something . . ."

"Yes?"

"Ghosts can't go through the Cerberus Catapult. At least not by themselves." Then he explained to her what would happen.

Sophie swallowed. "I'll speak to Cerberus," she said resolutely. "Maybe he'll let us through when I explain to him that you're trying to help me and you're not trying to escape."

Salabim shrugged his shoulders and hurried behind her.

# Sophie and the Secret Council of 12

Sophie's heart was pounding as she stood before the Cerberus Catapult. She was afraid of the huge mouth, but couldn't afford to lose any time. She had to act quickly! At least she hadn't run into the castle's heir along the way. Who knew what kind of evil spell he would have placed upon her! Sophie didn't doubt for an instant that he had also trapped Hammond with his magic. It was obvious that the heir wanted Ghost Park all to himself. It was possible that he wanted to use the ghosts and spirits to increase his power. Shivers ran down her spine. She was happy that Salabim and the Stone-Softener were nearby.

"Hello, Cerberus," she said loudly and clearly to the gigantic dog's mouth. "I'm Sophie, caretaker of the ghosts. I have to get back to the castle, together with both of these ghosts. They won't escape. They'll be under my protection. I need them. So, would you please let us through?"

She waited anxiously, but no answer came. Had Cerberus even understood her?

"Well then—I'll go in," she said and entered the dark mouth with shaking knees. Salabim followed her. He ducked his head and peered at the roof of the mouth. He expected the mouth to snap shut at any moment. But nothing happened. Sophie balanced on the huge tongue. She could almost reach the uvula. Abruptly, she stopped and gave the Stone-Softener to Salabim.

"Please hold on to him tightly."

Salabim's eyes flew open wide as Sophie lay down flat on the tongue and slithered cautiously toward the throat.

"What in heaven?" he called out fearfully. "Watch out! What are you doing?"

But Sophie wasn't listening. She was concentrating on her task. She crept forward on her stomach as far as possible. Before her, the throat opened up—a sinister red-and-black abyss. Somewhere down there Max was waiting.

Sophie cupped her hands around her mouth and yelled into the darkness, "Hello, Max. Can you hear me? It's me, Sophie. I'm going to try to get you out." Had Max heard her? She listened eagerly.

"He is very far down," mumbled Salabim behind her.

"Shhhhhh," she whispered, listening for an answer.

"Soooophie . . ." The voice was very far away.

"Max," Sophie screamed back. "Be patient. I'm trying. Just hold on." Then she slid back and stood up.

"That was quite brave," Salabim said appreciatively. "I wouldn't have had the courage myself. Cerberus would have only had to twitch his tongue and we would have slipped . . ."

But Sophie didn't need to be reminded of the danger. She reached up and tickled the uvula. Cerberus started coughing . . . and then all three were sitting in the entrance hall of the castle, in the middle of the pentagram. Sophie was light-headed for a moment.

Then she heard Salabim saying in awe: "Oh, what an exquisite lamp—I'd just love to have an apartment like that."

Sophie blinked and looked up at the huge chandelier, where countless crystals sparkled and glittered. Salabim was quite enchanted with the piece and appeared to have forgotten all else.

"Hey, pull yourself together," said Sophie, poking him in the ribs. "We have to get to Hammond's office." She stood up and took Boo-hoo's hand. The Stone-Softener was observing everything with wide eyes. But, luckily, instead of crying, he was just looking around curiously. Sophie headed straight for the office. No one was there. Hammond was definitely being held prisoner somewhere!

She sat Boo-hoo on the desk and went around to the other side until she stood in front of the computer and the phone. Before, when she had decided to alert the Secret Council of 12, everything had seemed so simple. But now she wasn't so sure. How could she contact this magic council? Could she just call them on the telephone? At the very least she needed a telephone number. She pulled open drawer after drawer, hoping to find Hammond's personal address book with all of his important addresses and phone numbers. But all she found were two packets of tissues, fingernail clippers, a rock-hard eraser, two pairs of sunglasses, a tin case with earplugs inside, a package of sunflower seeds, a highlighter, a bottle opener, two keys, a dust cloth, and a bag of cough drops.

Disappointed, Sophie shut each of the drawers. If Hammond indeed owned an address book, he must be carrying it with him. She could've screamed! How was she supposed to come up with the phone number?

Sophie stared at the telephone as if she could make it ring. That would be quite a coincidence, but it would definitely help her! One of the members of the Secret

Council of 12 could call at this very moment to talk to Hammond about the state of things.

"Oh," said Salabim suddenly, "I think I need glasses."

"Just keep quiet," growled Sophie. Salabim's complaints interrupted her concentration.

"But look at this . . . this book . . . it has very strange letters . . ." He laid a thick leather volume on the desk next to Boo-hoo. The Stone-Softener stretched his neck to see.

Sophie glanced at the book and assumed it was written in a foreign language. Then she stopped abruptly. Salabim was right. The book was odd—very odd! In fact, the letters were moving. They never stayed in the same place. Instead, they constantly changed positions. Sophie had just finished reading "ice and frost" when the words changed to "niced farost" and then "torid a incesf." She grew dizzy from the dancing letters.

"What kind of book is this?" Sophie reached out and closed it.

GOOK GHOISTBUDES—SELUR AND STIP was on the front cover. Sophie blinked and read the word again. TSOHG BUKOOGIDE—LESUR AND SPIT. She blinked again. GHOST GUIDEBOOK—RULES AND TIPS.

"I've never seen a book like this before," said Sophie amazed, as she leafed through it. Then a piece of paper fell out from between two pages with a note written in pencil: LICNUOC: 37-75-43-00-80. Sophie screamed with joy. "I've got it. LICNUOC—that can only mean COUNCIL."

Trembling with excitement, she grabbed the phone and dialed the numbers. She listened. The connection crackled, then a woman's voice said, "I'm sorry, the number you have reached is not in service . . ."

"Darn." Sophie hung up and thought for a moment. Of course! She had to dial the number backward. She grabbed the phone again and redialed. This time it rang and, after a while, someone answered.

"Yes?" said a man's voice.

"Is this the SCT?" stammered Sophie. She waited for the man to say, "Sorry, wrong number" or "Is this a joke?" but instead she heard, "Yes, that's right, central information."

"I . . . um . . ." Sophie didn't exactly know how to begin. "I am Sophie Stieger. I was just hired as a . . . um . . . ghost caretaker." That word sounded so weird! "Along with Max. Max Hope. Mr. Hammond hired us.

But something has happened to him. And something happened to Max, too. He's stuck . . . in the Cerberus Catapult . . ."

"Did he fall down?" asked the man as if she were talking about the weather.

Sophie nodded vigorously. Then she realized the man couldn't see her. "Yes," she said quickly. "But he was pushed. By this man . . . the one who inherited Ghost Park. He is totally mean and cast a spell on me and I was imprisoned in stones. The Stone-Softener and Salabim had to get me out . . ."

"Easy, easy, young lady," said the man on the other end. "Are you trying to say that right now everything is out of control in Ghost Park?"

"Exactly." Sophie was relieved that she was being taken seriously.

"Then I will summon a catastrophe conference," said the man.

"Please hurry," begged Sophie. "And save Max, please!"

"Listen," said the man on the other end of the line. "Go directly to the conference room. It's on the second floor. Go up the big stairs and then through the winged doors. You can't miss it. We'll be waiting."

Before she could ask any more questions, he hung up.

"I have to go to the conference room," said Sophie, putting down the phone. Then she noticed she was shaking all over. It wasn't everyday that she called the Secret Council of 12!

"Should we come with you?" Salabim asked.

"Of course," answered Sophie. "You are both my friends. And I would feel a lot better if I didn't have to stand alone in front of the Council . . ." She had begun to shiver.

Salabim noticed and put his hand reassuringly on her shoulder. "It will be fine."

"I just hope they can help Max," mumbled Sophie. She picked up Boo-hoo and they went looking for the conference room.

The conference room was enormous. Sophie entered and was surprised to see that no one was there. Curiously, she looked around. In a circle stood several short columns. Sophie counted 12 of them. On top of every column was a marble head—seven men and five women.

"We're the first ones here," said Sophie. Her voice echoed in the chamber. "I hope we won't have to wait very long."

"Oh, no," a women's voice said next to her. "We're already here."

Sophie spun around. One of the female marble busts had come to life. She no longer looked like white stone, but instead like a human. She had reddish hair, rosy skin, and eyes and lips that were heavily made up. Sophie felt the eyes of the sorceress on her and the red mouth smiled kindly at her.

"I am Albrun, I specialize in Elves and the Natural Spirits. I see you have a Stone-Softener with you. A very sensitive creature. Are you being very careful with him?"

"Of course," said Sophie and scratched Boo-hoo between the ears.

To her left one of the male heads came to life. He had a long beard.

"I am Kaan and am currently the head of the Secret Council. We just spoke with one another on the telephone."

"Oh, hello," said Sophie. She looked around, confused. "Are real people coming? Um . . . I mean . . . you are all just heads . . ."

"My dear Sophie, we magicians and sorcerers are strewn around the globe,"

explained Kaan. "To make a personal appearance would have taken much too long. We hold most of our conferences this way."

Sophie swallowed. "I see."

In the meantime, 11 of the 12 marble busts had come to life. Only one marble head stayed white.

"Typical Hjalmar, always late."

"Let's begin without him," said Albrun. "This is urgent business, right, Sophie?"

Sophie nodded.

"It would be best if you could tell us once more what has happened," Kaan prompted her.

Sophie began. At first her voice was trembling. She had never had to speak alone in front of so many grown-ups, and never in front of sorcerers and magicians. She briefly explained how she and Max had gotten the job. Then she told them about Boo-hoo and the letter from the heir. Finally she explained how they had looked for Hammond today, but hadn't found him, and how the heir had appeared and what had happened. She didn't forget to mention the part about the weird pant leg.

The magicians began to murmur until Kaan asked for silence. "Those are awfully severe charges against the heir of Ghost Park, Sophie," he said. "You are saying that the man wanted to hurt you and Max. And you also believe that he is holding

Hammond prisoner somewhere. It certainly sounds like Jonathan von Fleuch is unsuitable to undertake responsibility for Ghost Park and the well-being of all of its creatures."

Sophie was being tested. All 11 pairs of eyes were on her.

"Is it possible that you are just jealous?" asked one magician. "That you are worried about losing your job?"

Sophie felt her face turn red. It was true that she hadn't been thrilled when she had read the letter from the heir. But she had certainly not imagined Jonathan's imprisoning her in stone or pushing Max down Cerebrus's throat!

She remembered something else. "He wanted to catch Nelly," she said. "The timid little mermaid. Nock stabbed him in the hand with his trident, but he almost caught her."

Again they began to murmur. Then Salabim joined in. Until now, he hadn't said a peep, and during

Sophie's speech he had just nodded in agreement. "Anyway, he stinks," he said. "I can actually smell evil—even upwind!"

Now complete chaos broke out. All the heads were speaking at once.

"That is outright slander!"

"His father, Balthazar von Fleuch, was an excellent protector of the park."

"Nothing like this has ever happened in the entire history of the place!"

"I know that Balthazar would have done anything for his son!"

"The child is just showing off!"

"Stop!" yelled Kaan. "Silence! I must have silence! We are not getting anywhere. Sophie, we will return to your accusations later. But first, we must free your friend Max. Albrun, would you be so kind?"

Albrun smiled at him. "But of course, Kaan." She closed her eyes and began to sing a spell:

*Ghost Park, oh, Ghost Park,*
*From you Max must disembark.*
*Send a ladder, made of rope,*
*He will climb it full of hope.*
*Eleven hundred steps from the pit,*
*He will work hard; he will not quit.*
*Ghost Park, oh, Ghost Park,*
*From you Max must disembark.*

The hall was silent.

"And what happens now?" asked Sophie shyly.

"At this very moment, your friend will discover a magic rope ladder, Sophie," answered Albrun. "He'll have to climb for a while, but I'm sure he'll manage."

Sophie took a deep breath. "Are there really 1,100 rungs? So many?"

"Well, it doesn't really matter if it's one more or one less," declared Albrun. "There are actually 1,079, if you want to be precise."

How long would Max have to climb? Sophie tried to calculate it, but she quickly gave up. It was better not to think about it! She knew he would be able to do it!

"And now back to you," said Kaan, turning his head to her. "In order to find out if you have told the truth and if Jonathan von Fleuch is unqualified to care for the park, there is only one option." He paused. "We must ask Balthazar von Fleuch." Again, it was quiet.

Kaan cleared his throat. "We must agree. Such an important decision can only be reached as a group. Who is in favor?"

Sophie watched as five of the 12 marble heads turned black.

"Six votes yes and five votes no," said Kaan. "That means the majority are for waking Balthazar von Fleuch and asking his opinion."

Suddenly, the last marble head came to life, and Hjalmar appeared.

"I'm really sorry, everyone, I had so much to do," he explained, gasping for breath. "In my area there was an unnatural breeding of Wish-Fish reported. I had to do something about it right away." He looked curiously around. "Did I miss something important?"

"We were just voting," said Kaan a little impatiently. "It concerns Jonathan von Fleuch, the current heir to Ghost Park. This girl is of the opinion that Jonathan is completely unqualified for the task. We are considering waking Balthazar von Fleuch and asking him. What is your opinion? Yes or no?"

Hjalmar hesitated. "One should leave the no-longer-living in peace. That is my opinion. Only in the most extenuating of circumstances . . ."

"It could be that this is an extenuating circumstance, Hjalmar," said Kaan.

"No. I don't think so," said Hjalmar. "I am against it." His column turned black.

"It's undecided," Kaan declared. "Six for and six against." His gaze settled on Sophie. "What are your thoughts on the matter? Is it necessary and appropriate to wake Balthazar von Fleuch and ask him?"

Sophie's heart pounded. "I don't know . . . I mean . . ." She looked to Salabim for help. He nodded encouragingly. "I wouldn't trust his son with my life!"

"Are you prepared to face Balthazar and answer his questions?" Kaan asked in a serious voice.

A lump formed in Sophie's throat. "Yes," she answered; her voice no more than a whisper. "As well as I can."

"Good," said Kaan. "Then my authority as chair of the council breaks the tie. The Secret Council of 12 decides to question the deceased Balthazar von Fleuch. And Sophie will make the preparations."

# The Lord of the Castle–as a Ghost

When Sophie heard what she had to do, she thought she would faint. She was supposed to visit the Fleuch's family crypt. As soon as the ghost appeared, she would have to answer all his questions truthfully.

"You will not augment your accounts, nor will you leave anything out," Kaan advised her. "And in case Balthazar von Fleuch wants to see his son Jonathan, you will go together into Ghost Park."

"Th-th-th-through the Alley of D-d-d-dreams?" Sophie asked. She couldn't stop her teeth from chattering. The very idea that the ghost of the deceased castle's owner would be standing in front of her made her stomach ache. And she really had to use the bathroom, but she didn't trust herself to leave the room as long as the conference was still in progress.

"There are more gates to Ghost Park," she was told by Kaan. "In the crypt itself there is an entrance. You will use it." Sophie nodded. She hoped she could remember all of this! Kaan turned to the group. "Which of you wants to accompany the girl and speak the magical words? Albrun?"

But Albrun shook her head. "I don't know if I am able to remember the correct spell or not. And I wouldn't want anything unfortunate to happen."

"Omes? Guedlore? Adeodatus?"

But everyone declined the offer.

"Hjalmar?"

Even Hjalmar refused.

Kaan sighed. "Then I will have to do it myself. Sophie, I trust you with my head. Are you strong enough?"

"Huh? What?" It took a moment for Sophie to understand that she had to lift Kaan's head from the column and take it with her. She grew very pale.

"If you have a problem—I can temporarily change back into a marble head," said Kaan. "But you must consider that such a marble statue is quite heavy. I don't know if you can carry it." Sophie gave Boo-hoo to Salabim and walked up to the column. Tentatively, she took Kaan's head from the platform.

He winked at her reassuringly. "See, I told you. It's fine, right? Just something to get used to." Kaan was friendly, but still Sophie felt weird carrying the talking head under her arm. It was about as heavy as a pumpkin.

"What happens if I accidentally drop you?" asked Sophie.

"Same as if a marble statue fell on the floor—it would break. Nothing happens to me personally. You must remember I am hundreds of miles away. I'm simply using this head. Just as you heard my voice on the telephone, you are hearing my voice now—everything else is just an illusion. A little magical trickery, nothing more."

190

Sophie was somewhat calmed. "But the head feels so real," she said. "The hair and the skin—they're warm . . ."

"Well, we are all powerful magicians," said Kaan. "We make everything as perfect as possible. But if the warmth disturbs you, I can change it."

Immediately, Sophie felt the head under her arm growing cold as ice. But she found that even more gruesome. "N-n-n-no, please . . . please—I prefer it as it was before."

Kaan's head warmed up. "Hurry up now," he said. "If your suspicions are founded, then this Jonathan can wreak havoc. The sooner we get this matter settled, the better."

"Good luck," came the response from all sides.

"Thanks," said Sophie.

She left the chamber with the head, followed by Salabim, who carried Boo-hoo in his arms. As she went down the steps, she thought of Max. How many rungs on the ladder had he climbed so far? She hoped she would see him soon. Would they actually be able to bike home together this evening?

As they left the castle through the entrance—Salabim looked up wistfully at the beautiful chandelier.

Kaan directed her north. Sophie had never been in this part of the enormous garden. At the very edge, hidden by tall trees, was a small chapel. Steps led underground. There was a wrought iron gate at the bottom of the steps, which opened to reveal a room. The walls were roughly hewn from stone and had large niches, in which big stone sarcophagi lay. Tiny red votive candles flickered everywhere.

"The Fleuch's family crypt," said Kaan.

Sophie shuddered. She found the place anything but cozy and was horrified at the thought that shortly, the ghost of the castle's master would appear.

"You can set me down gently somewhere," said Kaan.

Sophie looked for an appropriate place, and then set the head carefully in a niche. Kaan smiled. "Thanks."

"Of course." Sophie was glad to be free of her burden.

"Which is the right sarcophagus?" asked Kaan.

Sophie studied the inscriptions.

"Ludwig von Fleuch, died 1799. That can't be it. Adalbertine von Fleuch, born 1813, died 1903. That's not it, either." Sophie turned the corner and bumped into Salabim, who was inspecting one of the lamps.

"Nice lamp, don't you think?" He held up a wrought iron lantern with yellow stained glass. But Sophie took no interest in the lamp. She was much too preoccupied. The next inscription was the right one. Balthazar von Fleuch was written on a new-looking stone coffin. At least, it wasn't as weathered as the others, and moss hadn't begun growing on it.

"Here he is," said Sophie in a hoarse voice.

"Very good," said Kaan. Then he started mumbling Latin words.

Sophie shivered. Her hands were damp with sweat and she regretted not going to the bathroom. What would happen now? Would one of the stone coffins open and the dead lord of the castle climb out—right in front of her? Involuntarily, she took a step back.

"*Pax cum dignitate*. Peace with dignity. But grant us just a few more moments, because an important matter must be cleared up. It concerns your son; it concerns the future of Ghost Park." Kaan ended his speech.

Sophie stared at the coffin. Nothing moved. Wasn't it working?

"Boo-hoo thinks the lamp is also pretty," said Salabim next to her, holding the lamp in front of her nose again. "You didn't even look at it very closely."

"Very cute," Sophie answered mechanically. Her gaze moved to the stairs leading outside, which were suddenly illuminated with light. She heard footsteps. Someone came down the stairs, a middle-aged man wearing a light suit. He was tanned and looked as if he had just vacationed on Majorca. At first, Sophie

assumed he was a member of the Fleuch family who had come to see the family crypt. What would happen if he discovered Kaan's head? And Salabim? And Boo-hoo? What was she supposed to say? There wouldn't be enough excuses! Sophie thought to herself.

"I come unwillingly, but since I was called so urgently, I do want to know what's going on. So, how can I help you, Kaan?"

Sophie was speechless. Was this the ghost of the castle's owner? She had imagined him completely differently. Much more sinister and older and paler.

"This girl, Sophie," Kaan's gaze turned toward her, "is complaining about your son, Balthazar. She maintains that he is unqualified to run Ghost Park."

"So, so," said Balthazar and turned to Sophie. "Would you mind telling me how you came to this conclusion?"

Sophie began to tell, first stuttering and embarrassed, but then her voice became stronger. She didn't forget a single detail.

Balthazar looked thoughtful. "The man whom you describe doesn't seem to be very competent."

"And he stinks," Salabim added, putting down the lantern and coming forward. "He smells awful, even upwind, from a mile away."

Balthazar wrinkled his forehead. "I haven't seen my son for a long time. But as far as I can remember, he is a sensitive person who has reverence and respect for all creatures. If the man in the park is my son, then he has changed! I want to see him. Come on, Sophie, show him to me."

"You want to go into Ghost Park?" asked Sophie.

"Yes." With an ease Sophie never would have expected, Balthazar lifted the stone lid upon which Ludwig von Fleuch was written and swung his leg over the edge. "This will take us."

Sophie hesitated.

"Don't be scared, the coffin is empty," said Balthazar. "It's a fake. There never was a Ludwig von Fleuch—at least not in my family."

"I see," said Sophie, relieved. She was about to follow

the lord of the castle when she heard Kaan behind her.

"And what about me? Have you already forgotten me?"

"Sorry," Sophie mumbled and grabbed the head with both hands. "And you guys?" she turned to Salabim and Boo-hoo.

"We'll come along, of course," said Salabim and climbed into the sarcophagus behind Sophie.

From there, a stone staircase led deep underground. The steps were narrow and slippery. Sophie held the iron handrail tightly. The walls around her shimmered green and gave off an eerie and unnatural light, much like the phosphorescent light of a glowworm. After a while Sophie wasn't sure how long they had been going down. The stairs seemed endless. Overhead, she heard a dull noise as the coffin's lid was closed.

At last, Sophie glimpsed a soft, shimmering light. Balthazar stepped through the opening first. Sophie and Salabim followed. A deep gorge stretched below, and a small path led into the distance. Ahead was a shape much like the carcass of a huge animal.

"The Cetacean Bridge," explained Kaan, who was still in Sophie's arms. "That is the way to Ghost Park. No matter what happens you must go on. Do not become distracted, no matter what you see."

That didn't sound very heartening! Sophie wasn't exactly eager for any surprises. She had had enough for one day. As she neared the bridge, she saw that it was actually the skeleton of a large whale. A wooden footbridge, extremely narrow, led from the tail to the mouth. The bridge looked far from trustworthy or steady. Luckily, there was a rope to hold onto. Balthazar went first, nimbly crossing the bridge as if it were the easiest thing in the world. Sophie followed slowly after. The planks under her feet swayed. The wooden bridge was moving! Frantically, she gripped the rope and wished she were already on the other side.

The gorge surrounding her was deep and dark. From far below came the sound of rushing water.

"Just remember," Kaan advised her again. "Keep going—no matter what happens."

Sophie was determined to follow the advice. But she had gone only a little way when her surroundings suddenly changed. As she gazed through the bones of the whale, she had the impression of being in the middle of the ocean. Stormy, high waves rolled toward her and slapped against the bridge. Above her, huge seagulls circled with greedy eyes and sharp beaks. Their squawking echoed in Sophie's ears.

"Go on," commanded Kaan. "They're just phantoms, nothing more."

Bravely, Sophie set one foot in front of the other. To her right appeared a black sailing ship. The mast was broken and the sails ripped. Without a helmsman, the ship was thrown back and forth between the waves.

A thought ran through Sophie's head like a shot: the *Flying Dutchman*. She remembered the saga of the ship that was cursed to sail for all time on the ocean. The crew was long dead—only their ghosts were on board.

Sophie tore her gaze away and went on. But suddenly she stopped. Before her on the path appeared a large hole. She could see the deep fathomless water below.

"Keep going," commanded Kaan. "Whatever you see is not there at all."

The next few steps took enormous effort. She was afraid to fall into the depths below. But then her feet felt the wooden boards. Kaan was right. In reality, the hole wasn't there.

As she continued across, a wooden board flew toward her, and then a dreadful, violet squid squatted in the middle of the bridge and stared at her with his single, hostile eye. Emboldened by Kaan, Sophie simply stepped through him.

Finally, she reached the other side. Salabim jumped down from the footbridge behind her.

"My goodness, my goodness!" he blabbered and put Boo-hoo onto his other arm. "What an awful bridge!"

Boo-hoo, who had closed his eyes during the entire crossing, carefully peered through his fingers.

The path before them led into a craggy, wild area with jagged cliffs and waterfalls. As she looked back the way they had come, she saw the Cetacean Bridge turn into an actual whale. It sank into the depths of the gorge, water crashing over it. But then the vision was gone. Only the gorge remained.

Kaan seemed to guess Sophie's thoughts. "Yes, the Cetacean Bridge is a kind of one-way street, just like the Alley of Dreams. You can enter Ghost Park this way, but you cannot leave. It is a precautionary measure, so that the ghosts don't flee."

As they continued on, Balthazar turned to Salabim. "What about your sensitive nose? You already said that you could smell my son a mile away. So bring us to him!"

Now Salabim took over as leader. Again and again, he stood still, held his nose to the wind, and sniffed noisily. First he would go left, and then he would go straight, but finally he went to the right. Sophie wrinkled her forehead. She wasn't sure if Salabim had exaggerated his sensitive sense of smell. But then, the genie stopped so abruptly that Sophie almost bumped into him.

"The man is very near," he declared and held his nose. "Phew, he smells like the plague!"

The group continued around a hill, and suddenly they saw Jonathan von Fleuch in front of them. He was standing at the edge of a pond, casting a fishing line.

"My dear son," called Balthazar. "Give me a hug." Jonathan, who hadn't noticed their arrival, gave such a start that he dropped the rod. It slipped into the water. He stared at Balthazar, dumb-founded.

"Who are you? What do you want from me?" he demanded.

"But Jonathan, don't you recognize your own father?" asked Balthazar and stepped toward his son. "I may be dead, and, of course, you are surprised by my appearance, but your memory cannot be that bad!"

Balthazar hugged Jonathan to him, but when he took a step backward, he held a dingy cloak in his hand. "Look here!" he called triumphantly. "With this the traitor tried to disguise himself as my son!"

Now Sophie saw how Jonathan had changed. He was heavy-set and round, with thin blond hair and a little pointed nose. He wore a red shirt and checkered pants, whose pattern Sophie recognized at once.

"A magical metamorphosizing cloak," said Kaan. "Anyone who wears it can take on any desired appearance."

"Unfortunately, the cloak has a hole," added Balthazar. "That's why the transformation wasn't complete and why the bottom of his left pant leg and his left shoe remained the same."

The fake Jonathan let out a cry and turned to run away. From under Sophie's arm, Kaan mumbled something. The stranger continued to run, but he didn't move from the spot.

"A simple treadmill spell," explained Kaan. "He can't get away as long as I don't want him to. I assume that in a while he will tell us what he has planned and who he is. And of course it will be most interesting to hear what he has done with Hammond."

Sophie could hardly wait. But suddenly she noticed something was wrong with Boo-hoo. The Stone-Softener had started to sob uncontrollably. He held tight to Salabim and wept more than Sophie had ever seen before.

# Ariel's Confession

Boo-hoo would not calm down, no matter what Sophie or Salabim said or did.

"Why is he panicking all of a sudden?" pondered Kaan. He glanced at the stranger who had finally noticed that his efforts to run away were useless. "Maybe you know the answer?"

"Make him go away," sobbed Boo-hoo. "Boo-hoo doesn't want to see him. He was mean to him, and made him cry—a lot! "

"Do you know this man?" Sophie asked quietly, scratching Boo-hoo's ears.

Boo-hoo sniffed, turned his head away, and pressed himself against Salabim's chest. "Ariel," he blurted out. "He is evil . . . very evil." He started sobbing anew.

"Ariel?" Kaan repeated. "So this man's name is Ariel?"

Boo-hoo nodded and hid his head behind his hands.

"Ariel . . ." Kaan thought for a moment. "Ariel . . . Ariel . . . Ariel Parasol! Of course! I knew that I had seen this face before."

Ariel stared at Kaan but did not say a word.

"The last time the Secret Council of 12 was elected— 12 and a half years ago—you were a candidate," Kaan said slowly, thinking it through. "You wanted to become a member, but you were unable to fulfill the requirements."

"Oh, that was a long time ago," Ariel replied with a scowl. "I would have passed the test, if only . . ."

"Would have passed?" Kaan repeated and raised his eyebrows. "You failed with the lowest score in history."

Ariel shrugged his shoulders. "I guess. Right now, I can't remember it that well."

"Then I will remind you," Kaan said. "Fiona is your grandmother, right? She was on the council with us for many years. An excellent magician, until she left of her own volition."

"Yes," added Balthazar. "A wonderful woman. And so aware of her responsibilities. She stopped because she realized that her magical powers were weakening. She didn't want to take any risks."

Sophie noticed how Ariel drew himself up as the two men spoke of his grandmother. "Now tell us where Hammond is!" Kaan demanded.

At first, Ariel didn't want to admit anything. But when Kaan threatened to turn him into a Snorting-with-Rage Ghost on the spot, he caved. "That man challenged me," said Ariel. "He acted like he was master of Ghost Park."

"But Hammond is master of the castle at the moment," Balthazar said to him. "He gave me his word before I died."

"Last chance—what have you done with Hammond?" Kaan repeated his question.

203

"As soon as this treadmill spell disappears, I can show you," replied Ariel tartly.

"Don't think that you can deceive us," Kaan warned. He mumbled a spell and Ariel could move freely once more. But they didn't let him out of their sight as he led them around a hill to a grotto.

"He's in there," Ariel said.

"The Grotto of the Ice Fairies," Balthazar observed.

"Ice Fairies?" asked Sophie.

"Creatures made of snow and ice," explained Balthazar. "They only feel comfortable in temperatures around zero degrees. That's why this grotto is as cold as a freezer."

Sophie swallowed. "Then is . . . has Hammond turned to ice?" She gasped. "He must be dead!"

"Calm yourself, Sophie," said Kaan. "Don't forget that everything works a bit differently here in Ghost Park. If Hammond has actually turned to ice, then the Secret Council of 12 can defrost him."

Sophie was relieved but still she was anxious to rescue the old man. As she stepped into the grotto, a wonder world of ice appeared before her eyes, and she shivered. She knew she wouldn't be able to bear the cold for very long, but the others didn't seem to mind the freezing temperatures. It even seemed as if Balthazar felt totally comfortable here in his summer clothes. Well— he was just a ghost!

Huge icicles hung from the ceiling. Others rose up from the ground. There were elaborate columns and other fantastic formations. But the most wonderful of

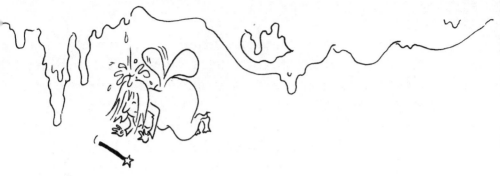

all were the ice fairies, who were flitting around the icicles. Sophie could only catch fleeting glimpses of the white figures. The timid ice fairies didn't let anyone near them. But Sophie could hear them whispering and speaking softly. Curiously, they watched as the strangers entered their grotto.

"He is in here," said Ariel and pointed to a thick ice column.

The ice column was completely opaque and looked like any other column in the grotto. One could've searched for Hammond for years without finding him.

"And how are we supposed to get him out?" asked Sophie.

The block of ice looked unimaginably heavy.

Kaan hesitated. "I'm not happy to do this. But just this once, I will break the rules. I will use magic to bring all of us, including this block of ice, back to the conference chamber. That is the quickest way."

As he shut his eyes, concentrated, and began to speak a few magic words, something occurred to Sophie. Something very important. She tapped him gently on the top of his head.

"And what about Max?" she wanted to know. "Since you're already breaking the rules—can't you use magic to bring him back, too?"

"All right, Sophie," Kaan sighed. "I'll make an exception. *Sic volo sic iubeo . . .*"

★ ★ ★ GP ★ ★ ★

Max had just reached the 633rd step of the rope ladder. His hands were already raw from grabbing onto the rope and his legs were heavier than lead. He didn't dare look down. How much longer did he have to climb? Would there ever be an end? Or was this just another trick of Ghost Park, a new ordeal?

At first he had been extremely happy when the rope ladder appeared. It was just in time, since the sea was threateningly close and the sandbank had shrunk to a tiny strip. Max was sure that Salabim had been doing his best to get help. For a moment, Max had even imagined that he heard Sophie's voice from far above. But he wasn't completely sure. So when the rope ladder had fallen in front of his feet, he could have screamed

206

for joy. Eagerly he had started climbing.

But after about 100 rungs, he began to have doubts. After 200, he had to take a break. After 300, he was quite discouraged, but there was nothing left for him to do except to keep climbing. After rung 400, he gave up hope, and with the 500th, he howled in frustration. Luckily, no one was there to see it.

Now he was unbelievably thirsty. For a quarter of an hour he hadn't moved from the spot, he simply didn't have the will to. The rope ladder seemed to have a million rungs. "Stupid Ghost Park," he mumbled. "I wish I had never come here! What a dumb world of phantoms and witchcraft!"

He sniffled and with one hand searched for a tissue in his pocket. Instead of a tissue his fingers bumped into something hard. The worrystone, which he had found during his first visit to the castle! The stone with the magic symbol had brought him luck more than once.

"Help me," whispered Max. "If you're really any good, then get me out of here!" He rubbed the stone on his pants and stuck it back into his pocket. As he grabbed for the next rung, he only felt thin air and much to his horror, realized he was sailing through the sky.

The ice block stood in the middle of the conference room and all the magic heads concentrated their gaze on it.

"Put me back on my column, Sophie," commanded Kaan.

Sophie was about to obey when suddenly Max appeared next to her out of thin air—with wounded hands and a haggard expression on his face. He looked around in disbelief. He was quite relieved to see Sophie again, but he couldn't explain at all what had just happened.

"Hello, Sophie," he grinned a little unsurely. "I don't know what's going on here, but thanks for getting me out! That stupid rope ladder just about brought me to my wits' end. But—eeewwww, why are you carrying someone's head around with you?" He made a disgusted face.

"This is Kaan, the chair of the Secret Council of 12," explained Sophie. She was delighted to see Max again. Later, she would tell him every single detail, but unfortunately she didn't have time for that right now. She did have to set one thing straight though. "We had to call upon the ghost of the castle's dead owner. Balthazar von Fleuch exposed Ariel as a traitor."

She placed Kaan back on the marble column. "The head isn't real. I mean, at the moment Kaan is somewhere else. This is just a marble head that Kaan speaks through."

"Hm," said Max, who still hadn't quite understood everything. Then he quickly jumped to one side, as a bright light suddenly streamed from 12 pairs of eyes onto the ice block.

In no time, the ice began to melt. A large puddle spread out onto the floor. Soon the center of the ice block was visible—Amadeus Hammond.

At first, the old man lay prostrate on the floor, then slowly he began to move, and finally he stood up, completely soaked and awfully confused. The beams of light were extinguished. "The Secret Council of 12 thanks you for your commitment and courage," said Albrun. "Through the bold actions of these two children, Ghost Park has been saved from the hands of a traitor."

"Oh," cried Hammond, looking at Ariel in bewilderment.

"So, Ariel," began Kaan boldly, "tell the council and our guests your story. But I warn you—we want only the truth. Lies are pointless. Your grandmother, the honorable magician Fiona, has been called."

Suddenly, on the wall across from the entryway, a picture appeared. It looked like a projection screen. An old woman with messy white hair gazed into the room. At her feet crouched a gray wolf, which she stroked with her gnarled hands.

"Greetings, Secret Council of 12," the woman called. "The cause for my visit is an extremely unfortunate one. I wish my grandson hadn't done this. I am so ashamed of him and ask all attendees to forgive his atrocities."

"Oh, be quiet, Grandma," said Ariel sullenly. "Stay out of this. It's my business."

"No, Ariel, don't be fooled," Fiona said. "It does involve me. Because you grew up with me." She turned to face the stone heads.

"Honorable Council, Ariel has lived with me since he was five years old. Unfortunately, his mother died early and his father never took care of him. Even as a child, Ariel was interested in magic and sorcery. I wished that one day he would follow in my footsteps, but I found out very quickly that he had absolutely no magical talent."

"That's a lie!" yelled Ariel furiously.

"Oh, no, it's true," contradicted Fiona. "In regard to anything having to do with magic, you are as untalented as a normal human. In addition, you are power-hungry and lazy."

Ariel looked as if he might explode at any moment. The members of the council began to speak loudly with one another. Fiona had trouble regaining her audience.

"I'm not finished," she called. "Ariel didn't accept that he would never be a sorcerer. Therefore he tried, behind my back, to gain knowledge from my secret magic book."

She paused for a moment, then continued: "That's

why I wanted to demolish the book. I placed the pages in a magical shredder, a so-called "shredding wolf," in the hope that they would be torn into tiny pieces. I wasn't quite finished when the apparatus turned into a real wolf." She petted the wolf that lay by her feet. "Yes, you're such a good boy!"

Fiona paused. "Honorable Council," she began again, "this is a demonstration of how hard it is to destroy magic books. I sealed the leftover pages inside my chimney in order to protect them from my grandson."

"You have always tried to stop me from having any fun," said Ariel, pouting.

But Fiona ignored him. "I advised my grandson to look for a respectable job in order to make a living. Ariel became a forester, and for a long time I was sure that something useful had become of him." She made a face. "Unfortunately my grandson was just waiting for the opportunity to deceive me."

"Don't believe a word she says," Ariel mumbled.

"One day, while working in the forest, he met a troll," Fiona continued. "It was a green forest troll with red eyes and seven toes on each foot. My grandson was able to influence the troll. He promised him a huge reward if he would catch a Stone-Softener for him. Because the tears of such a creature could burn through the strongest stone—even the stones of my chimney!"

Boo-hoo, who was still sitting in Salabim's arms, had been listening intently. Now he started sobbing again. His tears fell on the floor, but they had no effect on the oak parquet floor.

"The troll obeyed him," Fiona said. "One day he actually brought my grandson a Stone-Softener." She paused for a moment. "Must I describe to you how both of them tormented the poor creature? They teased him so, the little Stone-Softener couldn't stop crying. That's how Ariel came upon the leftover pages of my magic book."

Sophie felt incredibly sorry for Boo-hoo. Now it was obvious why the little guy was always crying. He had lived through something awful.

"With the help of the leftover pages and my ancient magic cloak, my grandson disguised himself as the heir to Ghost Park," Fiona continued. "Unfortunately, I learned of this too late or else I would have used any magic power I still have to hinder his plan. But I was sleeping as he stole the pages from the chimney. Just now my magic mirror, which had been watching Ariel, told me everything."

"Don't believe a word this crazy lady says!" screamed Ariel. "She hasn't been right in the head for a long time. If she were would she have a wild animal as a pet?"

"Oh, no, Ariel, you won't get away with this." Fiona stayed even-tempered. "I know that the Council will believe me. And this creature here actually used to be a magical shredder. He's become quite old. I almost believe he will change back soon."

"She's nuts," Ariel said. "It's obvious."

Fiona smiled and knocked on the back of the wolf. It sounded metallic. "Do you hear that, Council members? That's metal. Shortly, my wolf will become what he once was. His back legs are already quite stiff."

Ariel covered his face with his hands and shook his head.

"You've been convicted, Ariel," Kaan said. "Your grandmother has told the truth. We have no reason to doubt her words."

"She's lying!" Ariel insisted.

"Don't cause more trouble, Ariel," said Albrun. "You realized you would never be a sorcerer. And with the help of the magic book and the beings from Ghost Park, you hoped to obtain the power you sought—but your plan has collapsed."

The fake heir hung his head. It was obvious he had given up.

"Now you will give the Council every page of the magic book," ordered Kaan. "Each magician will receive a page and will guard it well."

Hesitently, Ariel took from his breast pocket a stack of papers. Balthazar distributed them around the circle. Sophie watched as the papers rolled together and slid under the heads. When the 12th page had disappeared Ariel began sobbing quietly.

"You will come home with me," Fiona said. "You will saw boards again and hunt for firewood. And in the future you will leave trolls, Stone-Softeners, and other magic creatures alone."

Ariel had to give a solemn oath to the Council that in the future he would steer clear of anything magic. In front of everyone, Balthazar tore up the magic cloak. It barely took any effort. The ancient fabric came apart easily. "And now this cloak cannot inflict any more damage," Kaan said satisfied.

Then—with a clap of thunder—Fiona and the wolf disappeared. A lightning bolt from the Council sent Ariel with her.

"This conference is ended," said Kaan after a moment. "It's been exhausting, and we will now retreat."

One by one, the 12 heads turned back into white marble. Then Hammond, Balthazar, Salabim, Boo-hoo, Sophie, and Max were alone in the room.

"I don't believe I am needed anymore," said Balthazar and smiled. "Luckily this adventure ended well. I am very happy that it wasn't my son who inflicted all that evil." He nodded at everyone, then walked into the wall and disappeared.

"Whew," sighed Hammond. "Do you know what I would really like right now? I'd like to get out of these wet clothes!"

A little while later, they were all sitting in the old man's office. Amadeus Hammond had changed his clothes and Boo-hoo was digging into a pile of socks and dipping them into a jar of mayonnaise. Max, Sophie, and Salabim sat around the desk and told Hammond each and every detail of what had happened while he was frozen inside of the block of ice.

"You have proven yourselves to be very capable ghost caretakers," said Hammond appreciatively. "Boo-hoo and Salabim were also excellent. I think you all have earned a reward."

Max and Sophie exchanged glances. Both knew that to be allowed to continue working at Ghost Park was all the reward they'd ever want. When they told Hammond, he agreed without a moment's hesitation.

"Boo-hoo wants another name," the Stone-Softener spoke up suddenly, wiping some mayonnaise from his mouth. "Boo-hoo sounds like a crybaby."

"We'll think of a nice name for you," promised Sophie, nudging Max, "won't we."

Max nodded. "We'll definitely think of something."

"I thought that Boo-hoo could even live in my office," said Hammond. "There's enough room in the filing cabinet. And then I'll always have company. Ever since Nepomuk, my little Clingy-Ghost, fell in love, it's been a little lonely here."

215

Boo-hoo beamed. He liked the suggestion.

"And what is your wish?" Hammond asked Salabim.

The Genie of the Lamp wrung his hands together. "I do have one wish," he said with hesitation. "But it might be a little brazen. I need a new lamp, and there's that beautiful chandelier in the entrance hall. May I live there?"

"If that's all," said Hammond, "then I don't see why not."

The group smiled as Salabim joyfully threw his turban into the air.

"We'd better start for home, Sophie. We'll have a lot of explaining to do when our parents see our math test grades," said Max.

Slowly returning to the real world, Sophie sighed. "Ugh, I forgot about that. Thanks a lot, Max, I feel like I'm back in the Alley of Dreams." Sophie sighed again as the two moved toward the castle door and their long ride home.